Blade's Pixie

Wolfsbane Ridge MC Book2
Marissa Ann

Credits:
Cover Design by: Francessca's PR & Designs
Editor: Rachel Goldman
Blurb: Melissa Mitchell

ASIN:
ISBN-13:

3

Author's Note

I want to thank everyone who has supported me with my writing. This will be my second release and it was so much harder than the first. Hopefully, this book is as amazing as the first. There are plans for release of future books in this series as well as the other MC's mentioned in Wolfsbane Ridge. Again, thank you all for everything!

Chapter 1

Blade

I have been in love with Bella Winters for years. There was only one problem; she wouldn't give me the time of day. At least she wouldn't until recently. We finally hooked up one night and I thought that it was a foregone conclusion that we were an item. But according to her hard-headed ass, it didn't mean shit. Even though our one night together resulted in consequences that I had no idea about until it was too late.

Ever since she was attacked, she hasn't allowed me close to her. It doesn't keep me from doing some stalker type shit such as sleeping on her front step and constantly having her watched by one of the prospects. She hasn't said anything directly to me about it but according to Fang, she let him know real quickly that she didn't appreciate any of it.

"Damn woman." I mumble under my breath as I head into the clubhouse to speak to my best friend and president, Timber.

When I reach his office, he is on the phone and doesn't sound too happy about whatever it is he is hearing. So I take a seat at his desk to wait, which doesn't take too long as he plops down into his own seat with a sigh.

"Problems Prez?"

"That was Officer Wilson on the phone. They found evidence at the warehouses that suggests the kidnapped girls were transported to

Louisiana. They may be in the same position that Bella found herself in." He says with raised brows.

"Fuck!" I say as I shake my head at the image. "What are we going to do Prez?"

"I think I should call my future in-laws and get them in on this since it is located in their territory. They have more contacts there that could dig up information that likes to remain hidden from outsiders."

"That's a good idea."

"I also think I will send you out to give them some help."

"I can't leave Bella right now Prez! Fuck! I just nearly lost her. Actually, she's further away from me now than she's ever fucking been!"

"You both need time Blade! And you ARE fucking going! I'll keep an eye on Bella. Every brother here will and you know it. She may be saying she's not but, everyone in town knows she is yours. It'll do you good to get away and clear your head. Go help out on this missing girls case. When you come back, Bella and you will both be more settled with a clear head."

I know that Timber means well and there is probably some truth in what he says, but I seriously don't want to leave Bella right now. Far as I know, no one yet knows about the baby. The baby we both lost.

"Okay, Prez, I'll go but only because you are making me. Just let me tell Bella that I am going. And; for the love of God, make sure she stays safe!"

"You can count on it brother. Officer Wilson will be going out with you in his own cage. He is taking some personal leave from the sheriff's office. I think it was pushed on him by the Mayor because of how close to the case he is. They know he's going to Louisiana, but he has been ordered to turn over anything he finds to the feds."

"Well, fucking hell!! You mean I got to watch out for those bastards while out there too? Come on Timber, this is getting even more fucked up!"

"I know that it is but I have a firm suspicion that Reaper can help out as far as the feds are concerned. His MC has been in that territory for a really long time and with that comes connections that we will need."

"I'll head out in an hour after I talk to Bella. Or I should say, try to talk to Bella."

"She still won't speak to you?"

"Not a peep since the night we rescued her and Mina." I sigh and rub my neck as I can feel a headache coming on. "I'll call you as soon as I get there and check up as often as possible. Keep me updated on Bella. I have a feeling she's gearing up to act out as soon as I am out of sight."

"You know I will Blade. Good luck out there and if you need anything, call me. I can be out as soon as possible if needed ." Timber says as he shakes my hand and I walk out the door headed to see the girl I love that refuses to love me back.

Bella

I can hear the motorcycle way before I can see it. I know exactly who it is. I haven't spoken one word to him since I told him about the baby that night. I know he blames me, I could tell by the way he shut down on me as soon as he found out. He left the room and didn't come back for hours. He claims he loves me but if he did, he wouldn't have left me in my grief.

I don't look up as I hear him coming up the front steps but I can see the toes of his boots.

"How are you doing Bella?" He asks but I continue to stare at the toe of his boots. He let's out a long sigh.

"Fine, you don't have to talk, just listen. I'm going out of town for awhile. Not sure exactly how long I will be gone but when I come back we are working this shit out. I'm more than tired of the silent treatment."

I try not to react to his words, although it is like a knife to the heart. How can he run off like this after everything we have been through? What I have been through?

"I'll call and text you every day. I really hope you answer because I will miss you *Pixie*. I love you so very much; I have for a really long time."

"STOP!! Just stop saying you love me Blade! I am sick of hearing you lie to me!! Just run off to God knows where and leave me the hell alone!" I scream at him as I run inside.

10

A few minutes later I can hear the sound of his engine as he roars away. I am sure in that moment that everyone in the county can hear the sound as my heart breaks into a billion pieces.

My mom comes back from the store a little while later and I can hear her moving around in the kitchen. I pray she leaves me alone for just a little while longer.

Everyone hovering over me since the attack is about to drive me insane. It's making me think about doing something drastic, like taking a nice long vacation without telling anyone, if I could just figure out a way to slip past the prospects…

****

"I'm dying in this fucking heat! And the mosquitoes are big enough to pick me up off my bike!"

"Sounds rough as hell, man, glad it's you and not me." Timber says during our daily phone call.

"I'm telling you, you've never felt heat like this shit. I'll be surprised if my balls survive all the chafing!!"

"Bella probably wouldn't like it if you lost your balls while there!" he says while laughing his ass off at me. The fucker!!

"How is she anyway?"

"She seems to be getting back into her normal routine. Mina headed over to the café just a little while ago to visit with her and give Fang a little time off from his post. I had an errand I needed him to run. He should be back before Mina leaves and the shop closes for the day."

"I'm glad she's getting back to her normal self."

"I wouldn't exactly call what she's doing, normal. Yes, she's doing all the things she did before but she never smiles and has refused to run the front counter at the café."

"So who is running the front counter?"

"Her mom for right now but she has posted an ad looking for an employee."

"Are you looking into all her possible employees?"

"Of course we are Blade. She's using the agency in town and they are giving me all the information on possible candidates before Bella even sees the applications. Stop worrying. You know we take care of our own and that includes Bella."

"I know Prez, but she still won't answer my calls or texts, so I worry all the time since I am not there."

"Anything happens and you know I will call you."

"Yeah, I know. So, is there any new information on your end?"

"I talked to Reaper earlier today. He said you should check out a little dive bar called Gator's Dunk. He said it's out in the bayou where the law isn't likely to go and where most anything underground can be heard about. He has a contact there that should be expecting you."

"What's the guy's name?"

"Surprisingly, it's a woman. She goes by the name Firefly." He says as he laughs a little

"Fucking seriously?"

"Serious as hell."

"How will I know it's her?"

"Reaper said you'll know by the huge flame tattoo she has crawling up her right arm. And Blade?"

"Yeah Prez?"

"He said not to piss her off. Something about her being the reason his cabin burned down couple years ago."

"She burned his fucking cabin down?"

"Yep, with him passed out drunk inside of it."

"Classic! I wonder how he pissed her off." I say while laughing.

"I have no idea and I damn sure wasn't about to ask. I have a feeling the two of them still have some unfinished business between them though."

"I wouldn't want to ask either. I'll head over to the bar tonight and see what I can find out. I'm sure Officer Wilson will want to tag along."

"Just don't let him get too much in the way. At heart, he's still a law man even if he is on a little vacation."

"I'll call later tonight if we find out anything. Later." I say as I hang up the phone.

I click on a new text message to send to Bella. Although she never answers, I do know she reads them. I just wish like hell she'd talk to me!

****

I've been planning, watching and waiting for couple weeks now. Just waiting for a chance, one slip up on the MC's part that will allow me to slip away unnoticed. I think today just may give me my chance.

They think I don't know that they've been having all my potential employees going through Timber before I even see their applications. But I do know. I am not that damn stupid to believe that they are only having me followed around by the prospects. And I now consider Mina a traitor as well, since she seems to be helping them keep close eyes on me.

Their slip up today may not be of their own making though. I have a little help in that department. I know a little red head from down the way that is sleeping with Dane. I paid her a little cash to send a message to Mina at an exact time from Dane's phone to make her think that I have a new watcher. I plan to be far away before they realize what has happened.

"Bella, are you even listening to me?"

"You know what Mina? I am tired of hearing the same bullshit from all of you about Blade. Besides, none of you know the entire story."

"Then talk to me Bella! Tell me what is going on with you! You've been tight lipped ever since that night. I know something more went down. It will help you to talk about it. I am your best friend for Christ sake! Tell me what is wrong!"

"It doesn't matter, its over with now. I just want to forget that night ever happened."

"Damn it Bella!" she says to me as her phone pings with a new message.

Hopefully this is the message I have been waiting for her to receive. I have got to get the hell out of this town for a while.

"Guess I'll go since you won't talk to me but I'll be back tomorrow. You have got to release whatever it is that is eating you up inside." She says as she heads towards the door.

"Mina…"

"Yeah girl?"

"I really am sorry for not being ready to talk, not even to you. Just trust me when I say that as soon as I am ready, I will call you." I say trying to get her to understand.

"Okay Bella. I will always be here whenever you are ready."

As soon as she leaves, I grab my purse and head out the back door where I parked my car early this morning. I have had a bag packed and in my trunk for a week now waiting for my chance to get away.

I look around the parking lots and roads as I head North out of town. If I go in that direction before circling back South to hit the main highways, they can't track my movements to see what direction I went in. I put away enough cash so that they couldn't track any of my purchases as well.

17

You would think I was running for my life with the way I have had to do things. I just know they would put a tail on me and not leave me completely alone. This is just something I need for myself right now. I need different scenery and people who don't know who I am around me. I need time to come to terms with everything I have been through. With what I have lost.

Once I figure it out, I'll call Mina. I'm not worried about my coffee shop; Mom will take care of everything. She's been amazing through it all and surprisingly has yet to ask any questions. It's like she knows I will talk to her when I am ready to do so. Normally she is all up in my life driving me insane.

Once I put all signs of White Summer Montana behind me, I let out a huge sigh of relief. I'm the only car on the road and I'm finally free.

****

A few hours after talking to Timber, Officer Wilson and I pull into the bar called Gator's Dunk. I can't help but shake my head at the sight in front of me.

The bar is basically a boathouse with a wooden bridge going out across the water and there are definitely real alligators in the water beneath it. There's only one sign that says "Watch Your Step". Good luck to any fool that gets drunk before walking back across that rickety old bridge.

"Good Lord, We are walking across that?" Officer Wilson says as he walks up next to me.

"Yep, is there a problem?"

"No problem son, just don't let my old ass fall over the side." He answers back.

"First of all *John,* don't call me *son.* Second, if you are not feeling up to it, stay your old ass out here in your car. I have no time to be babysitting your ass. If it had been up to me, I'd have tied you to a chair and did this on my own." I say as I walk towards the bridge.

I have no idea what the hell Timber was thinking sending me out here with Officer Wilson. He knows I hate all cops. The hate I hold for them all, it's a part of me just as my blades are an extension of my hand. Mother fuckers never did anything for me but cause trouble.

"Look Blade, I mean no disrespect to you when I call you son. I know a little bit about your background. I'm truly sorry for what all you probably went through as a kid. Can we try to get along while we are here? You never know, you may decide by the end of this to call me a friend." He says to me as I am walking towards the bridge.

I know he's going through his own shit right now with his niece still missing. I just have a hard time not picturing his badge when I look at him.

"Just come your old ass on. You fall in though; you are completely on your own. I hear that gator's love fresh pig." I reply as we start across the bridge towards the front door of the bar.

The inside of the bar is dimly lit and absolutely full of shady looking mother fuckers. Most of the women walking around look as if they have never stepped foot inside of a shower.

"Holy hell." John whispers as he takes a look around. It's one of the very few times I have ever even heard the man utter a curse word but it causes me to grin in his direction.

"Be careful in here John. No telling what you could accidentally pick up."

"Yeah, like rabies!" he mutters back at me making me chuckle.

"Come on; let's get a seat at the bar. Maybe I can spot the little lady from there and hopefully the beer isn't too bad."

We make our way to the end of the bar so that I can position myself to watch the door which has always been my habit. I learned a long time ago that it was a good habit to have. My mother's third husband taught me that lesson very well. He was one mean son of a bitch.

As soon as we sit down, the bartender takes our orders and brings us both a beer. It actually tastes better than I'd hoped it would.

"Did Timber not get any other information on this girl other than a flame tattoo up her right arm? I mean, what if she's got it covered up? How will we know who we are looking for then?" as soon as John asks that, a voice from behind us answers.

"Because I never cover the mother fucker up, I'm too proud of it."

We both turn around to see a pretty little thing with a flame tattoo up her right arm. I honestly don't know what I expected, but she definitely doesn't fit whatever I had in mind. She's petite; with long, curly, dark brown hair and eyes so blue they almost appear translucent.

"You must be Firefly?" I ask.

"And you must be Blade the little shit head said to look for." She answers.

"I don't know very many, if any, who'd call Reaper a little shit head to his face or behind his back."

"I'm not scared of that mother fucker and he knows it. Besides, he has had plenty of chances to try and kill me. He hasn't done it yet, he's not going to either."

"Sounds like a pretty long history between you two."

"You could say that but I doubt it's the type of history you are thinking about. I have known him since I was in diapers."

"But you tried to kill him in a fire at his cabin?" I ask, getting even more confused about their history.

"That wasn't the only time I tried to kill him." She answers sweetly while smiling. I'm starting to think this chick may be a little crazy. "Enough right now about all that shit, fill me in on the situation and I'll see what I can do to help you brothers out."

"To tell you the truth, we don't have a lot to go on. Some of the local girls back home are missing and all the clues lead back to some voodoo shit here around New Orleans."

"I need to know what kind of voodoo shit you are talking about to get an idea of where to start. There are a lot of different things here in New Orleans, from freaky ass shit to down right nightmare shit. So anything you can tell me, no matter how small a detail you think it is, can help point us in the right direction." she says back to me.

I kind of feel uncomfortable sharing this shit with her. I'm not used to women like her that seem to know how to deal with the crazy shit that can be found in this fucked up life.

"Did Reaper get a chance to tell you that his sister and her best friend was kidnapped couple months ago?"

"Holy fuck, are you serious? Is Mina okay?" she asks.

"She's actually very well. She was only bruised up a little. It was her best friend, Bella, which nearly didn't make it. I'm not sure what kind of voodoo bullshit it was, I can only tell you what kind of shape Bella was in when we found her. Are you sure you are up to hear these kinds of details?"

"I've seen a lot of shit so don't worry about my female sensibilities, I don't have any."

"Damn woman, what the hell in your life has made you so hard?" Officer Wilson asks.

She cuts her eyes over to him and says, "You wouldn't believe me if I told you. Besides, we don't have enough time for all of that. What did these guys do to this Bella chick?"

"When we found her, she had small cuts all over her arms and legs, bruises from the top of her head to the soles of her feet. But the truly weird part is that they drained nearly every drop of blood from her veins without actually killing her and she was covered in blood. That blood wasn't the blood from her body though. The best they could come up with at the lab was that it was cow and chicken blood."

"The cuts on her body, were they in any type of design?"

"I wouldn't call them a design really, they were more like precision cuts in exact locations. The middle of each palm, the middle of the stomach, middle of both feet, was all exact locations. All other cuts seemed to be exactly two inches apart. They were not deep enough to leave true scars when healed though."

"Sounds like some of that new age shit that has been showing up in the streets of downtown."

"So, you've heard of this type of voodoo?"

"Yes, I have and usually the girls do not live to tell what happened to them. There's an old voodoo shop run by a woman I know really well. She could probably cough up a name of someone in the know about this new occult. Everyone goes to her for all the best ingredients to do their magic."

"When could we meet with her?"

"The shop opens at 8am. It's called Rosie's, meet me there at 7:30 in the morning." She says as she checks her phone. "I gotta run, I'll see you there."

"Later." I say back as she rushes towards the door. I look over at the sheriff who has stayed quiet. He looks like he's going to either shit himself or fall out in the floor. "You okay there John?"

"I'll be fine in a minute. Let me finish this beer before we go."

"No problem." I say as I can tell he really does need a few minutes. I pick up my phone to text Timber and find several texts from him already. I open them up and as I read them, I am filled with worry but also anger. Bella has run away from home like a damn child and no one has any idea where the hell she is.

Chapter 3

Bella
Two Weeks Later

I've been traveling back and forth across the states, never staying in one place for long. I'm still constantly watching my back to see if the MC has picked up my trail. I turned my cell phone off before I ever got out of White Summer so that they can't track me with that.

I'm currently crossing Arizona. It's absolutely gorgeous here but seriously the absolute silence around me has started to take its toll.

"What if this car breaks down out here? What ya going to do then Bella? Other than keep talking to yourself." I say out loud and shake my head at myself.

Yeah, I definitely need to find somewhere I can stay and hide out for a while. Being alone is all nice and good, but humans need other humans.

"It needs to be a crowded city and I need to be able to get a job that pays in cash." I say to myself. I'll keep going until funds get really low and hopefully by then I will have found a place.

****

"Any leads on the name you got from the woman at the voodoo shop?" Timber asks over the phone.

"Yeah, we got a call that he was found stabbed to death at a motel just outside the city that is known for prostitution. We are headed over that way after we meet up with Firefly. We are hoping one of the whores will be willing to talk to us. I also talked to Reaper. He said his contact with the Feds will meet us there but will keep a low profile so the girls are more willing to talk."

"I really wish we could wrap this shit up already. How's Officer Wilson doing?"

"He's holding up well; guess that cop training comes in handy sometimes. Do you have any word on Bella?" I ask.

"Her cell phone still hasn't been on. She's being smart on that one. She also hasn't contacted anyone here in White Summer, not even her mother. Wish she knew how badly she is worrying everyone. I may just whip her little ass like a child when we finally find her."

"You'll have to get to her before I do. I certainly plan to tan her hide for this shit!"

"Well, call me when you have anything new on this occult."

"Sure thing, Prez." I reply before hanging up.

I'm still standing in the same spot thinking about Bella when John walks up next to me.

"Any news about your girl?" He asks.

"Not a damn thing! I swear she was put on this earth to drive me fucking crazy. I almost think she does the shit on purpose. She's been doing it for years!"

"Of course she knows son! Women learn that fine art before the age of two!" He chuckles at me. "We ready to head out?" He asks.

"Yeah, let's go. Firefly is supposed to meet us in an hour."

****

We pull up to the hotel a little while later and can see Reaper's contact standing next to a bike.

"Doesn't look like a Fed to me. But he's definitely pretty." Firefly says causing John to start chuckling in the backseat.

Pretty wasn't the word I would have used. He looked like he had stepped off the cover of one of those magazines you see at the grocery store.

"Let's just hope he has some brains behind that pretty boy face of his." I say as he heads in our direction.

"Officer Wilson, I'm Agent Fox Richards."

"Nice to meet you sir. This is Blade with the Wolfsbane Ridge MC and this little lady is Firefly."

"Nice to meet you both." He says as he shakes our hands.

"So what do you have?" I ask him directly.

"The last prostitute he was seen with is a young girl named Tammy. She's currently in room 208. She would be our best source of information because it appears from the months of surveillance, she was his favorite whore. All the girls here know him as Slim but his real name was Jake Knowles. His wrap sheet is more than a mile long." He explains as we walk towards room 208.

She opens the door after the third knock and I am surprised to see a girl that looks to be around sixteen years old.

"Can I help you?"

"We just want to ask you a few questions about Slim if that is alright? We will pay you for your time."

She looks at all of us very slowly before she opens the door wider to let us in. The inside of the room is fairly clean although the air smells like stale cigarettes.

"What do you want to know?"

"Did he ever talk about anything he was messed up in around you?"

"Not usually."

"What about any names of his associates? Did he ever slip up and say any of their names?"

"Only once and that was the night his body was dumped here. Earlier that day he was on the phone with someone named Aaron. I don't know if that is a first name or a last name as he kept calling him Mr. Aaron.

I overheard them talking about some girl whose family was looking for her. He was screaming at Slim about how the girls were supposed to be from broken homes that wouldn't go out of their way to look for them." She pauses in talking to light a cigarette and takes a long drag on it.

"I've never seen Slim scared before but he was scared after that conversation. He left out of here as fast as he could. Said he'd be back later. Only later winded up being his body thrown from a truck as it skidded back out of here."

"Do you have any idea about where he went or could have went?" I ask her.

"I really don't. You guys should go now. Customers will be rolling in soon."

"Thank you for talking to us." I say as I lay several hundred on her coffee table. As we walk out the door, she calls out to us.

"Why is it so important to know where he went that night? You guys don't seem like cops so I doubt that is why you are asking." She says to us all.

"We are looking for his niece." Firefly says while pointing at Officer Wilson. "She was kidnapped from her own house. All we want to do is bring her home."

"I don't know where he went that night but there was another night that I was with him. He said he had to stop somewhere before we went to the club. It was an old warehouse out on 23 in Belle Chasse. He made me stay in the truck while he went inside."

"Thank you Tammy."

"You all just be careful. These guys he ran with? They weren't the type you wanted to come across unprepared."

One Month Later
Bella

I've been in Memphis, TN for a while now. I accepted a job waiting tables for straight cash. The owner didn't seem to mind paying me that way, seems he is used to immigrants that need jobs but do not have a social security number. I suspect though that he thinks I am hiding from an abusive relationship.

I have no plans to correct him because I really need this job. I have always wanted to visit and see Graceland. Of course, I have also wanted to see where Elvis was born and raised in Tupelo, which is only a few hours south of here but that is entirely too close to Mina's brothers. They'd rat me out to Blade in a New York minute if they found where I was at.

I do miss talking to Mina though. I might just buy a burner phone and give her a call, just to let her know I am okay. At least they won't be able to trace the call.

Three hours later and my shift is finally over. I ran down to the corner store and bought a phone like I had planned. Now my nerves are getting the best of me. I know as soon as she hears that it is me, she is going to bitch me out like she never has before.

The phone rings several times before it connects. "Hello?" she answers in a hesitant voice.

"It's me." I say back and hold my breath waiting for the explosion from her.

"Bella? Oh my God!! Where the hell have you been? Are you okay?"

"I promise I am fine girl. I just needed to get away for a while."

"Where are you? I don't recognize the number."

"It's a burner phone and I am not telling you where I am. Just know that I am fine and safe where I am."

"Seriously Bella? You ran away like a little child, not telling a soul where you were going and months' later you call to say you are fine! You have everyone absolutely worried sick about you! Poor Blade can barely concentrate on what he's doing because of worry over you!"

"I really do not care how poor Blade is doing." I say back in a very calm voice even though I do not feel calm at all.

"Bella, please just tell me where you are so that I can come get you. Or how about I come out and stay with you? We could hang out, just us girls."

"You and I both know that wouldn't work. Timber would never let you go without at least a prospect with you at all times and I currently have no desire to be around the MC Brothers. Not a damn one of them!"

"Well hell Bella, will you at least promise to call me and check in? At least that way we will all know you are still alive!"

"I promise that I will call you. No one else though. I am not ready to deal with anyone else."

"Okay Bella, I love you sista'! You are not supposed to just go ghost on me like that."

"I know. I am sorry and I love you too. I missed hearing your voice which is why I called you. I've seen some amazing views so far while traveling."

"So you've been going pretty much non-stop? Timber told me that you haven't used any of your credit cards or withdrawn any money from your account. You are doing okay money wise?"

"Yeah, I'm good. Don't worry. You know I would call if it got bad."

"I hope so. I really hope that you know you can call me no matter what you need. And if you really feel like you need to stay away for a while longer, I will keep it secret of where you are if need be."

"Thanks Mina, you are the greatest friend I could have ever asked for."

"No problem chica. Just stay safe!"

"I will. I promise! I'll call you again in about a week. I need to get some sleep."

"Alright. Good night!"

"Good night." I say back as I hang up the phone.

My new boss also gave me a place to sleep. It isn't much, just a cot in the storage room. It'll work for now.

****

"So she called Mina?" I ask, clearly frustrated but relieved to finally know that she is okay and not hurt in a ditch somewhere.

"Yeah. Mina called right after to let me know. She wouldn't tell Mina where she was and apparently she used a burner phone so that it couldn't be traced."

"I am surprised Mina even told you she called her."

"I'm not. My girl and I don't keep secrets. Although she did promise Bella she wouldn't tell any of us where she is at if she told her. I've reached out to several of our brothers in other states to keep a look out for her."

"Let me know soon as any word comes in about her location. I plan to go wherever she is at; hog tie her ass and keep her next to me."

"We'll find her soon. She'll make a mistake or be recognized somewhere by another brother. I assume you have new information and that is why you have called?"

"We talked to the prostitute that Slim kept on the side. She gave us a new lead on an old warehouse in Belle Chasse. We are meeting up with the New Orleans chapter of the Night Howler's to work out a plan to put this place under 24 hour surveillance."

"Just stay safe and keep me updated. I'm going to put in some more calls to the nomad brothers that are scattered. Maybe it'll help find Bella." He says as he hangs up the phone.

A few hours later we are at the clubhouse of the New Orleans chapter of the Night Howler's. Skeeter is the President of this chapter but he still answers directly to Reaper.

"Reaper said to be sure none of you fuck this up. We need video and audio feed coming from the warehouse. If you can't get inside, get on top of the fucking building and go through the roof! We need to be able to see if those girls are there and how we can get in there to get them out safely. And above all, do not get caught! We don't want to tip them off." Skeeter tells his crew as they pack up all the equipment they will need.

"Where will the live feed come through at?"

"Come right this way Officer Wilson and I will show you." Skeeter says as he heads down a hallway.

We walk into a room that is filled from the floor to the ceiling with computers. There's one man sitting behind a desk tapping on four different keyboards as we walk further into the room.

"This is Buzz. He is our resident computer programmer." He says as Buzz throws a hand up as a way of saying hello but never stops tapping away on the keyboards.

"He can speak. You usually can't get him to shut up but when he's in his zone you'll think he doesn't hear a word you say. He'd probably knock the sweetest ass known to man out of the way of his precious keyboards."

"Find me a sweet piece of ass and we'll put it to the test." Buzz replies back but never looks up from the keyboard, making us all laugh.

"Skeeter, the boys are ready to head out."

"Thanks Mick. Buzz will use the drone to keep a look out."

****

Several hours later, the guys are all coming back in having completed the mission without too much fuss. Only one of the guys was spotted but he took the guy out before he could warn anyone else. They took the body to be disposed of leaving no traces of the Brothers ever being there.

The video feed coming through the computers has left us all speechless. There are girls in nearly every room on beds and hooked up to IV's.

"Doesn't take much to come to the conclusion that what's in those bags isn't just fluids. All the girls are too still. None of them are trying to get away." Buzz says in a soft voice from his computer desk.

"It's locked up tight. All the video feeds are coming from the air vents from the roof. We'll definitely need explosives to get through the doors." Mick is in the middle of saying as we watch one of the dickheads on the screen walk up to a girl on a bed.

We all get closer to the monitors to see what he is doing. We can only watch in horror as he pulls the girls dress up above her waist and pulls his own pants down. She never resists which

35

tells us that its a safe bet they are all being drugged to keep them quiet.

He mounts her and starts rutting like he's in a race. All I can do is watch her face. She looks to be in her early twenties with blond hair and a face that gives her more of a babydoll look. Cleaned up, she is probably a very gorgeous young woman.

His rutting finally comes to an end as he pulls out and zips himself back up. All I want to do is reach through the screen and cut his dick off.

"These fuckers need to die." Officer Wilson says from beside me. I look over and I swear I can see tears in his eyes.

"Oh, they'll die alright. Every mother fucking one of them!" Buzz says as he pushes back from his desk and storms out of the room.

Skeeter notices we are all watching Buzz walk out and says, "His baby sister was raped and murdered four years ago. She was only sixteen and the only blood family he still had left."

"I know that after watching that we would all like to go in with guns blazing but we need to plan this all out carefully. We need to watch for patterns in their routines. If there are times when the girls are left alone longer than others or if there are times when there are less of those fuckers to deal with.

The hardest part about all of this is going to be dealing with the feds. Fox was there when you were told about the warehouse. We need to make sure they also don't jeopardize all of this. I'll call Reaper so he can deal with Fox."

****

"This is some really fucked up shit Timber. Having to see that fucker doing that to that girl and no way of doing anything about it."

"Sounds fucked. I talked to Reaper. He said he's loading up the guys to come that way as soon as he finishes some business in Memphis."

"Yeah, he should be here by the end of the week. By then we should have all the intel to be able to get in there and get those girls out."

"Snake and Blood will be joining you down there by the end of the week as well. Do we know yet if one of the girls is Officer Wilson's niece?" Timber asks.

"Nah man. It's hard to make out any of the girls faces clearly. I just hope she's not one of the ones being raped while knocked out cold by God knows what kind of drugs they are being force fed through those IV's."

"I certainly hope not as well. All those girls will need plenty of help after they get out of there."

"Yes they will." I say on a sigh. "Any news about Bella?" I ask. Hoping with every fiber of my being that my sweet pain in the ass girl is alright.

"There's been no leads Blade. I'm sorry I don't have anything to tell you on that."

"It's not your fault man. I just hope that she is alright."

"I'm sure that she is fine. She will turn up eventually. Probably in the most unlikeliest of places."

"Yeah, well, as soon as we wrap this up, I am going to look for her. Soon as I find her, I am wrapping her in my arms and only letting go to whip her little ass." I say as Timber starts to laugh.

"I'll call you in a few days when Blood and Snake get down there." He says as we hang up.

"So your girl is missing?" Firefly asks from behind me. I never even heard her walk up.

"Not that it's any of your business but she ran off just after I left to come here."

"What did you do to make her run off?"

"What the hell makes you think I did anything?" I ask, getting pissed off that she's sticking her nose into my business.

"Seriously? You men are so stupid."She replies while shaking her head at me and giving me a pitying look.

"What?" I ask.

"Stop and think with your head. If a girl runs off, its definitely because you did *something*. You just got to figure out what exactly that something is." She says as she walks away.

"Why do you women have to be so damn crazy?"

"Because you dumbass men make us that way!" She replies without ever looking back.

"What the fuck has gotten into her." I ask myself.

****

Several hours later I'm outside smoking a cigarette when a bike pulls up to the main clubhouse. I can't make out who it is until he pulls his helmet off and I can clearly see that it's Buzz. I can tell he's a lot calmer than he was earlier when he stormed out of the computer room. But what I notice as he steps towards the light is that he's covered completely in blood.

"Holy shit man, are you alright?" I ask as I step towards him afraid that the blood is his. But that's a lot of fucking blood to still be up walking around. He looks down at himself as if he is only now noticing all the blood on himself.

"I just took care of some business is all." He replies as Skeeter walks out the door.

"What the fuck have you done Buzz?" Skeeter asks as he notices all the blood as well.

"I'll tell you all everything but first let me go clean up." He says as he continues to look at his blood covered hands.

"Fine. Go get a shower. But you better not tell me you've done something to jeopardize this fucking operation! It's taken too damn long to find out where those girls were being held and I mean to get them the fuck out of that hell they've been living as soon as possible."

Buzz just nods his head at Skeeter as he walks into the clubhouse.

"You don't really think he'd do something to mess all of this up do you?" I ask Skeeter.

"I don't think he would on purpose. But Buzz has a serious anger problem that's hard for him to control."

"What do you mean, hard to control?"

"He blacks out after a certain point and most of the time he can't remember doing things. He just *wakes up* to the after math. Which is what I suspect has happened this time. The guy we watched rape that first girl on the bed? He left that building and hasn't been back."

"Well I can't blame him if he took that fucker out as long as there is no mess to clean up, no body to be found and no way to trace it back to the club."

"Trust me when I tell you that if Buzz takes them out, no one will ever find a single hair from their heads." Skeeter says as he heads back into the clubhouse.

I stay outside a while longer smoking another cigarette and thinking about what may have went down with Buzz.

There really is no way I can blame him if he took that asshole out. The guys in the MC might do a lot of shady shit at times but one thing we definitely never do, at least in our club. We never hurt women or children. In other clubs it may not matter much, but in ours it'll get you taken out by your own brothers.

My thoughts turn to Bella. I hate not knowing where she's at and if she has a warm place to sleep. The doctor at the hospital gave her some vitamins to take. I just really hope she's taking care of herself.

Chapter 4

Bella

I've been on my feet all day from pulling a double shift. We don't close until 2am and it's still only 10pm.

"Hey Bella, tables three and four just filled up." Brian, the bartender and owner of the bar says to me as I come from the back room.

"Yeah, I got it." I say as I start to walk in that direction but am stopped by a hand that grabs my arm. I automatically stiffen up as fear races down my spine just as it has ever since the attack.

"Bella, I was hoping you were still working." Phil says as I turn to look at him.

I met Phil the second night after I started working here. He's asked me out on more than one occasion and seems to be getting even more agitated each time that I turn him down.

At first glance he seems like a very nice looking, well dressed guy. Someone any woman would absolutely love being on the arm of. But I sat back an observed how he treats others, and I completely can not stand him.

"Let go of my arm Phil." I say while looking at where he has a hold of me.

"Now sweetheart, don't be like that. I just wanted to see if you wanted to get together later after you get off work."

"Why can't you accept the answer I have already given you? I said that I am not interested." His grip on my arm tightens as I finish speaking.

"No one tells me no Bella."He says with gritted teeth. "I've let you pretend to not be interested as I know that's what women like you want but enough is enough. You will leave with me after your shift."

"I said no!" I say as I jerk back from him and head towards the tables to take their order.

I never once look up from my notepad as I walk towards the tables because Phil got my nerves so agitated. And truthfully, he scares me. It's not a surprise when I run smack into someone's chest.

"I'm so sorry....Oh shit." I say as I look up into eyes very familiar to me.

"Fancy running into you Bella Winters." Reaper replies with a smirk on his face.

I know that I am in trouble now as there is no way he is going to allow me to get away. He's going to call Timber and I'll be forced to go back to Montana.

"What are you doing here? Is Mina with you?" I ask as I pretend to look around.

"You know damn well Mina is with Timber back in Montana. Where you are supposed to be. But from what I hear, you ran away without telling anyone where you were going."

"Reaper, I am begging you. Please don't tell them I am here. I just needed to get away for a while. Get my head back on straight."

"Well, I hope you got it straight enough because when we leave tonight after I finish up my business meeting, you are going with us. Do not even think to argue with me about it!" He says as I open my mouth to do just that. "Where have you been staying? We'll need to get your stuff. We won't have any problems from your new boyfriend now will we?" He asks while looking in the direction I just walked away from.

"A room in the back. And he's not my boyfriend!" Is all I can reply as I just give up. Might as well go back with them. I think I am ready to say my peace to Blade any way.

"Well he's certainly looking at you like you belong to him."

"He's just a guy that keeps asking and I keep turning him down."

"Really? Well, don't worry about it, we'll be leaving shortly anyway. Spark will help you get your stuff." He says as I realize that Spark and a couple other guys had walked up behind me. Yeah, there really was no way I was getting away from them.

"Reaper, is there a problem?" Brian says from behind the bar. I had no idea that they were familiar with the Night Howlers here.

"No problem Brian, but this little lady is my sisters best friend that ran off a while back. They want her back home as soon as possible." Reaper answers while looking right at me. "You had to have known you were in our territory Bella and would have ran into one of us eventually."

"Actually I had no idea. How big is your territory any way?" I say as I narrow my eyes at him for laughing at my expense. Although I am more pissed at myself for not finding out more details about all of this shit from Mina.

"Spark, help her round up all of her things. Get one of the other guys to get her cage. No way are we letting her drive. I'll go finish this up so we can head south."

"Sure thing." Spark says as Reaper walks back towards the tables.

A little later, we are finishing getting all of my stuff back into my car. Spark has been pretty quiet the whole time. I haven't felt like talking anyway.

"Did you really think no one would eventually find you Bella?"

"I was hoping I could go back in my own time. When I was ready. When will we be going to Montana? Or will Timber send someone to pick me up you think?"

"Actually, we are headed to New Orleans on Friday. Got some business down there. But for now we are headed back to Tupelo to get some sleep." Is all he replies as he shuts the trunk of my car. The rest of the guys walk out of the bar and head towards their bikes.

"Who am I riding with?" I ask.

"You can ride with Spark." Reaper says as the bikes all start up at once.

The sound from so many bikes is a very familiar sound to me and immediately puts me at ease. I hop on behind Spark as all the bikes pull out from the parking lot. I wonder what is so important in New Orleans? As I look back at O'Neils Bar one last time. I can see Phil standing just outside the back door watching as we drive off.

44

"Reaper and his crew are due in sometime today." Skeeter says as he walks into the room.

"Good. I'm ready to get this shit over with." I say as I remember the several times we have had to watch several of those fuckwads on the screen rape some of the girls in that warehouse.

"We are all ready to get this shit over with." Officer Wilson mumbles from the chair he is sitting in.

He has been more quiet lately the more that we have seen of what is going on in that warehouse. For his sake, I hope we recover his niece without too much psychological damage to her.

As for Fire, she's been more agitated lately. Especially any time someone mentions Reaper or his crew.

I walk over to the table where she is sitting with Officer Wilson and Agent Fox who are talking to each other as she types like crazy on her phone. She turns it face down as I sit down next to her.

"Are you okay? You have seemed far away lately." I ask her directly.

"Oh I'm fine. Just have some family stuff I am dealing with. Thanks for asking though."

"Family is important. No one would think less of you if you needed to go for a little while."

"I said it was fine Blade. Deal with your own shit and stay the hell out of mine." She says as she jumps up from her seat and walks out the door.

"Damn it's easy to piss her off. No wonder she tried to burn down Reaper's cabin with him in it!" I say to the guys.

"I remember that." Agent Fox says.

"Really? Do you know why she did it?" I ask him.

"All I know is that it had something to do with her sister, Jade. Everyone was pretty tight lipped about it so I am not sure what it was."

"If she hates him so much, then why does she still answer him when he calls?" I ask as Agent fox looks at me like I've grown an extra head.

"You seriously don't know?" He asks as he takes a drink of his beer. I just shake my head at him.

"Know what?"

"She's part of the MC. She's married to Spark." He says surprising the hell out of me. "When the shit went down with her sister, she packed up and left Spark behind. I'm not sure where the sister is but they both left at the same time."

"Well hell, no wonder she's in a mood." Officer Wilson comments as Skeeter joins our table.

"Just got off the phone with Reaper. They should be here in another hour or so. And Blade? He says he found something that belongs to you and that you'll owe him one for returning it."

46

"What the hell was he talking about?" I ask clearly confused.

"I have no fucking clue. It could be anything with that crazy mother fucker. He was being all mysterious and shit." He says laughingly.

"Guess I'll know when he gets here. I'm going to go check on Snake and Blood. They were changing the oil filter on Snake's bike." I say as I head outside to the shop next door.

****

Two hours later I am still in the shop with the guys. We finished up the oil filter for Snake and were just standing around drinking a beer when I heard the roar of bikes coming into the lot.

"Sounds like Reaper and his crew are here." Blood says from his spot on the floor.

We hear the crunch of boots coming to the door before it swings open and see Skeeter there.

"Reaper needs you Blade." He says with a smile on his face.

I give him an odd look as I wipe my hands off and head out the door. I see Reaper and his guys all standing outside but as I get closer I can hear a female voice. At first I think it is Fire talking to Reaper but then I recognize the sweet voice of my dreams. She's arguing with Spark about going inside.

"Isabella Winters!" I say with a roar and everyone goes quiet. As I walk into the group, all the guys part like the sea to reveal my girl. She's standing in the middle with her shoulders back and a majorly stubborn set to her face.

"Come here!" I say as I point to the spot directly in front of me. She stands there several seconds without saying a word. "Do not make me come get you Bella!"

She finally stomps over to me and puts her hands on her hips.

"Who the hell do you think you are to demand a damn thing from me?" She asks.

"I'm the man that you fucking belong to! And it's time that you learned that fucking fact!" I reply back.

"Like hell!" She says as she turns to stomp away. But I don't give her the chance.

I throw her over my shoulder and start for the main clubhouse. Heading to the room that I have been staying in lately.

Of course she's screaming at me to put her down, calling me a barbarian and hitting me in the back the whole way. Several of the guys start laughing but I ignore them. It's time that she learned that I am the only man for her and that she is mine damn it! She has been since I laid eyes on her years ago.

I walk into my room and lock the door before I put her down on the bed.

"I have some things to say Bella and you are damn sure going to fucking listen."

"Why the fuck should I listen to you?"

"Watch that language woman!" I say back as she knows that I don't like when women use that kind of language.

"Why should I? You say those words!"

"It doesn't matter what men like me do. We are barbarians as you so kindly called me a few minutes ago but you are a lady and will act like one!"

"Whatever! Just get on with it so I can get away from you!"

"You won't be going anywhere Bella! You will have eyes on you at all times. I can't trust you not to run off again. I'm going to spank your ass like a child for pulling that shit! Did you once think about what you put everyone through?"

"Everyone was fine and I checked in with Mina."

"What if something had happened to you? No one would have known where the hell you were! You may have checked in with Mina but you sure as shit didn't tell her where the fuck you were at! We had the whole network of brothers in every state looking for your little ass!"

"I needed time to myself Blade! Away from everyone and their constant reminders of "poor Blade"!" she says with a smartass tone especially when she said my name.

"How can you not get how fucking much you mean to me?" I say back in a calm voice.

"Mean to you? How much did I mean to you when you were messing around with Vivi? Just how much did I mean when you wouldn't even look me in the eyes after we found out I had lost the baby?" She asks as a single tear runs down her face making my heart hurt for her all over again. "Why do you blame me for our baby's death Blade? I blame myself enough."

I slowly walk over to her and gently grab her face.

"How in the world have you gotten it into your head that I blame you for our baby's death? I couldn't get to you in time Bella. If its anyone's fault, it's mine." I say as I kiss her forehead.

"As for the Vivi thing. I didn't mess with her."

"I seen you in the kitchen Blade. She was in your lap and you were kissing her!" She says as she tries to pull away but I stop her.

"No little Pixie. She heard you coming down the hall and plopped down in my lap. She kissed me before I had time to react. I didn't even know you were standing in the door until later. I thought for sure you'd know I would never do anything like that to you. You are the only girl for me Bella Winters. I've been trying to tell you that for years but you just refuse to get it through that thick head of yours."

"I don't know what to think Blade."

"I'll give you time to think about it my little Pixie. But if you think I am letting you go, you'd be badly mistaken. I know you are meant to always be mine. Eventually you'll realize it as well. Now, are you ready for your spanking?"

"Oh no you don't!" she says as she begins to back away from me.

"Oh yes little Pixie. I owe you a spanking for the shit you have put all of us through by not knowing where you were."

I make a grab for her as she tries to dart towards the door around me. Sitting down on the bed with her draped over my knees, I slide her jeans down over her perfect little ass. An ass that I want so badly to bite that I start to get hard from just the thought and her wriggling around isn't helping at all.

"Be still Bella!" I demand as I start to rub my hand over the curve of one of her ass cheeks. "Damn, how I've missed this ass!" I say as I quickly raise my hand and it comes back down with a loud smack.

She jerks and immediately begins squirming again, trying to get off my lap. But I continue rubbing the spot I just spanked.

"Please Blade." She says in a small voice.

"I'm not hurting you Bella. But its time you learned who you belong to." I say as I quickly smack the other check and start to rub the spot.

After a few more times, I can hear a change in her breathing and know that she's starting to get aroused. While rubbing the last smack, I run my hand down the crack of her ass straight to her core and find my girl is soaking wet. She begins to moan as I gently stroke all around her pussy, rubbing all her juices over her clit.

"My baby likes getting spanked." I say and she just moans even more. "Oh yes, my sweet little Pixie loves this. Seems I'll need to find another way to punish you sweetheart."

I move her to the bed face down and continue to rub her core while I reach into my nightstand for the strips of leather I know to be there. I grab both of her hands and tie them together before tying them to the headboard.

"What are you doing?" She asks breathlessly.

"Making sure you stay put while I attend to some business little Pixie. But first I just need one small taste." I say as I lift her hips so that she is on her knees and move my face down until I can smell her sweet honey scent.

She starts to say something but cuts off as soon as my tongue drives straight into her pussy. I curl it back and forth several times causing her to moan and push back onto my face. She's wound so tight that I can feel how close she is to cumming all over my tongue. But I want her begging and I want her admitting that she is mine so I pull back away from her.

"Oh my God, Blade, what are you doing?"

"I have business to attend to. Don't worry, I'll be back." I say as I get up from the bed.

"Seriously Blade? You're just going to leave me like this?"

The look on her face shows disbelief but I've never seen her more beautiful. Her cheeks are flushed and her eyes bright with desire.

"Yes I am but don't worry, I'll take care of you." I say as I glide my index finger from her clit to her ass very slowly making her shudder. I can see her pussy glisten as it gets even wetter when I touch the core of her ass.

"Oh yes my sweet Pixie. I will definitely take care of you.....but later." I say as I start towards the door . I can hear her screaming at me all the way down the hall as I head towards the bar area.

Fire and Spark seem to be in a heated discussion in the far corner of the room as I walk in, so I go over to where the other guys are standing around.

"I don't know why he won't just divorce her ass." Reaper says while watching his brother. "Hell, they don't even live one day a year as husband and wife!"

A few minutes later Fire storms out of the clubhouse and Spark walks over to the rest of us.

"Get the bitch under control?" Reaper asks.

"Don't start your shit Reaper. She's still my wife."

"Not like you can tell she is. Y'all don't even see each other."

"And who's fault is that big brother?" Spark asks as he pushes past Reaper and walks toward the computer room. Reaper watches him walk away before following him into the room. A few minutes later Officer Wilson and I follow behind them.

Chapter 5

Bella

I struggle with the straps holding my hands to the bed for about twenty minutes before I finally give up and just lay there. My ass is still up in the air the way it was when Blade walked out. My clit still entirely too sensitive to touch the bed. If I don't get some relief soon, I'll probably scream down the roof.

I'm uncertain how long I lay there but eventually I let my legs slide to either side of me. The roughness of the top blanket on the bed feels so good on my pussy that I can't help but rub against it.

My rhythm starts getting faster and I can't help but to moan into the pillow under my face. I am so into it that I never hear the door open and shut. I only know that he is there when his hand comes down hard on my ass.

SMACK!

"Oh my God Blade, Please!" I beg him as the blanket just isn't finishing the job.

"As soon as you say it my love. Tell me who you belong to and swear you'll never run away again." He says as he gently brushes a finger along my wet slit.

"Mmmmmm." Is all I am able to get out through my throat.

"Say it Little Pixie so I can give us both the relief that we need." He says as he slowly undresses and starts rubbing himself slowly while watching my movements on the bed.

My mouth starts to water while I am watching him. I have always thought it almost unnatural the way my body responds only to him. Ever since that first night, he's been the only one that could play my body like an instrument that was made especially for him.

He climbs onto the bed behind me and starts rubbing me from my thighs, up over my ass and around to my breasts, barely pinching my nipples.

I moan and push my ass back into his cock trying to find the friction that I need. One of his hands moves down, gently stroking me. The second his fingers find my clit, he pinches and my body ignites like it's on fire as he slides his cock completely into my pussy in one stroke.

"Always so tight for me sweetheart." He says through gritted teeth as he holds himself back.

"Please Blade." I quietly beg as I push back even further on his cock causing us both to groan.

He leans down kissing up my back until he gets to my ear and whispers, "I need you to say it sweetheart, please." He moves just the smallest bit making my pussy squeeze even tighter. "Please Little Pixie, tell me who this pussy belongs to."

I'm wound so tight, just wanting him to move. To send me over the cliff to sweet oblivion. At this point I am certain that I would tell him anything he wanted me to.

"You Blade! She belongs only to you!" Before I can even finish the sentence, he slides nearly completely out before slamming back into me.

He builds a punishing pace as if he is trying to slam himself as deep into me as he can possibly get. But I do not care. I need him to fuck me hard. I realize that I have more than missed this, missed him.

"Oh God Blade, I'm going to cum." I say as he grabs a hand full of my hair and at the same time pinches one of my nipples.

"Then cum all over this cock baby. Cum now!" He says as he slams into me even harder.

"Oh shit!" I scream as my pussy gushes all over him at the same time as his cock swells even more and fills my insides with warmth. I cum so hard that I'm sure that I black out.

When I open my eyes again, I feel like I can't move and my body continues to twitch. He stays connected to me, wrapping his arms around me as we lay in the bed.

"You are mine Bella. You will realize that soon enough and admit it. Go to sleep my love."

I don't protest as I all of a sudden feel completely exhausted. But just before I fall into a deep sleep I swear I hear him say, I love you Bella.

The next morning I wake up before Bella and slip out of bed. I want to check in with the guys to see if we are ready to make plans about getting the girls out of the warehouse.

As I head towards the surveillance room, I see Fire talking to someone at the front door in hushed tones. I silently walk in that direction, extremely curious as to who she is secretly conversing with.

"You know better than to come here Jade! Especially with him here right now!" She says to what appears to be another woman at the door.

"I know Megan but my phone stopped working and I need you to be able to pick Amber up from school today. They are letting me pick up extra shifts and I really need it right now."

"No actually you don't need those shifts. I have offered to help you out but you act like money from your own sister isn't good enough for you."

"That's not fair Megan! We are not your responsibility. Amber is not your responsibility, she's mine."

"She's not just yours though, is she?" Fire answers back causing her sisters eyes to slit in anger.

"You promised not to tell him!" Jade says just before she finally notices me coming up behind Fire. Fire spins around pinning me with a look meant to freeze me in my spot.

"What the hell Blade! Sneaking up and eaves dropping on private family conversations now?"

"Didn't mean to over hear *Megan*." I say back with a grin.

Fire turns back to her sister and says, "I don't know what you expect me to do with her. I have to be here right now."

"I can ask Bella to watch her. How old is she?" I ask while Fire shoots daggers at me with her eyes and her sister looks hopeful.

"Amber is three. She's a pretty quiet kid so she shouldn't be any trouble." Jade finally answers.

"She'll be fine with Bella. My girl used to babysit everyone's kids back home."

"You sure she'll be willing to do it?" Fire asks.

"Absolutely, something about kids makes her already sweet heart melt even more. Besides it'll keep her busy while we conduct other business." I answer back.

"Thank you so much!" Jade says as she pushes her sister out of the way to give me a hug. "I gotta get to work now." She says as she walks away.

"Sweet girl." I say as Fire shuts the door.

"Yeah too sweet sometimes." She says back. "Look, don't tell any of the guys but especially Reaper that she was here please. He doesn't need to know and most definitely don't tell anyone who Amber really is while she's here."

"Any particular reason I should keep all these secrets to my self?" I ask looking straight at her trying to figure out the whys.

"It's family stuff that needs to be worked out within the family."

"I'll let that explanation work for now. But at some point I want the real reasons." I say as I walk away.

I walk into the surveillance room where all the guys are standing around a table looking over maps of Belle Chasse.

"We need to be sure and position guys at every point of entry into that warehouse. We don't want any of them slipping out and getting away to do this shit again." Agent Fox Richards says out loud.

"How do we know that the guys there is all that is involved? There has to be a bigger player they are getting these girls for." Buzz says from his seat in front of his computers.

"He has a point. There's no way they are just collecting these girls. They have to have a bigger purpose for them than to just have in a warehouse to use as they please." I say as I walk over.

"We realize that and that is why we are hoping to find records inside that warehouse after we get the girls to safety." Reaper responds back.

"So basically we will be up shit creek without a paddle if there are no records to be found?" Fire asks with disgust in her voice.

"We have no other way Fire. You seen how hard it was to even locate the girls. If Slim

60

hadn't messed up by taking his favorite whore with him one night, we'd never been given the tip about the warehouse. And I am sure that if they knew she had been with him one of those nights, they'd have offed her as well." Spark replies before his brother has a chance.

"So how long before you think we can go in to save the girls?" Asks Officer Wilson.

"At least a few more days. I want to be sure we have a very set and clear plan here with very few mistakes made." Agent Fox says.

"Afterward, Buzz will clear up all the surveillance tapes so that they don't show who exactly took these guys down. It'll look like a group of vigilantes went in. No one will ever be able to connect this to the clubs." Skeeter says as Buzz nods his head.

"That will wrap everything up nice and tight for the Bureau. Giving us just enough evidence for the scum in the warehouse to serve a life sentence at least." Agent Fox says.

"Alright, I'm ready for breakfast!" Buzz says as he jumps up and heads out of the room leaving everyone else behind shaking their heads at his quick 180 from the current situation.

****

I wake up to the smell of bacon and see a plate of food on the nightstand next to me. A movement across the room has me looking in that direction to see Blade putting on his shirt. I can tell he just got out of the shower from his still wet hair.

"Good morning sleepy head." He says as he walks over and kisses me on my forehead.

"Morning." I mumble back as I raise up and grab the cup of coffee.

"I brought your breakfast before I got a shower so it may be a little cold now."

"It'll be fine. Thank you." I say as he smiles back at me.

"You don't mind looking after a three year old later today do you?" He asks surprising me by his question.

"I don't mind but who's child is it?" I ask.

"Well that my Little Pixie is a complicated question." He says and I just raise my brow waiting on him to continue.

"This child in a way is related to Mina. Her aunt is a woman connected to the club that goes by the name of Fire."

"Oh you mean Mina's sister in law?" I say as I start eating my breakfast and surprising him for a change.

"You know about Mina's sister in law?" He asks.

"Of course I do. Mina and I tell each other everything. Besides, Fire would call Mina every once in a while to check in."

"Well hell, do you know about Fire's sister?"

"Not really. I remember only one time Mina mentioning a girl while on the phone with Fire. Her name was unique."

"Jade?" he asks.

"Yeah that's it. But they didn't speak about her for long. It seemed like a pretty heated conversation that ended quickly."

"Well this child belongs to Jade. She needed someone to watch the little girl while she works a second shift. I told her that I didn't think you'd mind doing that for her. I know how much you always enjoyed babysitting. So do you mind?"

"No I don't mind. I'd enjoy that very much. Besides, it'll keep me busy while locked up in this room." I say shooting him my best glare.

"Don't start that shit. You don't have to stay in this room but you will not leave the premises without someone with you. I can't trust you to not run off again."

"Blade, about last night? It changes nothing." I say to him.

"You think it changes nothing Bella but it does. It's proof that I am the only one for you, no matter how pissed off you think you are over something that wasn't what it seemed. I'm going to see if any of the guys need help in the shop. And let me make something clear...........I do not

nor have I ever blamed you for our baby's death."
He says as he leans down to kiss me before
walking back out the door.

After I finish my breakfast, I'm going
through my clothes so that I can take a shower
when my phone rings. It's been so long since I
used my regular phone that it makes me jump.

"Hello?"

"I waited as long as I could before calling
chicka! Now tell me exactly where my brother
found you." Mina says causing me to smile.

"I guess you want the entire story?"

"From the very beginning!" She says back
to me. So I sit back on the bed to tell my best
friend about everything.

****

Blade

I work with the guys in the garage until around noon but took frequent breaks to go check on Bella. She seemed to be doing just fine, she was in the kitchen talking with a couple of the guys ole lady's while they cooked the last time I was in there.

They ran me out of the kitchen when I tried to snatch a bite from a pot. One of them even smacked me with a spoon.

Most of the guys have already headed in to eat lunch when a small car pulls up. I can tell that it is Jade, so I walk towards her and help her to get her little girl out who surprisingly comes to me with all smiles. It only takes me a second to realize how very much she looks like someone I know.

"Amber this is Blade. You be sweet for him and his ole lady, okay?" Jade says to her before kissing her on the head.

"Yes mommy." She says back in the sweetest little voice that causes my stomach to clinch thinking about what my own child's voice would have sounded like.

"You sure about this Blade?" She asks me bringing me back from what if's that I shouldn't be thinking about.

"Yeah, It's not a problem. I asked Bella as soon as she got up. She's super excited about."

"Okay, well my number at work is in her bag there and of course Megan can get in touch with me if there is a problem."

65

"I can't believe her name is Megan." I say on a chuckle.

"Yes well, she'd prefer if I called her Fire like everyone else. But I grew up calling her Megan and that is what I will call her whether she likes it or not!" She says as she climbs back into her car. "I should be done at work around eight or so."

"That's fine. little Amber here will be well looked after."

"I know she will. I've heard my sister and Mina talk about Bella before. I feel like I know her already. I better get back to work. Thanks again." She says as she drives away.

I look at the little jewel in my arms who hasn't stopped smiling at me.

"Ready to go see Bella?" I ask.

"Yep!" she replies back as we head inside.

We find Bella back in our room digging through her stuff.

"Lose something?" I ask as we walk in.

"I can't seem to find my address book. It's just disappeared." She says as she looks up and then stills. "Wow, she looks like......"

"My thoughts exactly." I reply back knowing she is thinking like I was. That this tiny bit of a girl looks exactly like Mina.

"If we noticed it, then I'd bet anything Reaper and Spark will too." She says.

"Well they left a little bit ago. With any luck they won't get back until her mom picks her back up. Fire didn't say anything about keeping her hidden though."

66

"Are you ready for lunch Amber?" Bella asks her.

"Yes please!"

"Oh how very polite you are!" Bella answers back while picking her up and heading out the door towards the kitchens.

"Blade come?" she asks in that sweet voice.

"Yes sweetheart, Blade is coming too." Bella answers for me but never looks back to see if I am following.

That's because she already knows that if she ordered me to walk off the top of a skyscraper I'd do it without question. I love her so very completely that I'd do anything as long as she wanted me to.

Chapter 6
Bella

Later that night I am in the kitchen helping the other lady's cook dinner. little Amber is sitting on the counter helping Renee put icing on a cake. It actually looks like she has more icing on her tiny little face than on the cake itself.

I've had a lot of fun watching Amber this afternoon. It's made me think a lot about my own baby and what it would have been like to be a mommy. To do all these things with my own child every day.

Those thoughts of course lead me back to thinking about my relationship with Blade. I really do love that man regardless of anything we have been through. When I close my eyes and imagine my future children, he is there beside me.

A little while later after we have filled the tables with food and put the plates out, everyone starts coming in to eat. Amber stays right next to me the entire time. We are both sitting down to eat ourselves when Blade, Reaper and Spark walk through the door. Blade sits next to us and begins to fill his plate.

I look up just in time to see Reaper staring at little Amber. He has made no move to fill his plate and his brother looks in our direction to see what he is looking at.

"Blade, who's child is that?" Reaper asks while never taking his eyes off of her.

"Umm, well..." Blade starts to answer.

"She's mine." The answer comes from the door and we all look back to see both Fire and Jade coming through the door.

"Mommy!!" Amber says before climbing from her chair and running straight into her mothers arms. "Me miss you." She says in a sweet voice before kissing her mother on the cheek.

"I missed you too Love Bug." Jade says back to her daughter. "Bella, do I owe you anything for watching her?" She asks me directly.

"Not at all Jade. It was completely my pleasure. If you need my help again while we are here, just let me know." I answer back.

She looks back towards Reaper and Spark who have both been completely quiet before she turns to her sister saying goodbye and walking out of the door.

Fire looks back towards the table before grabbing a plate and sitting next to me in the chair Amber left. Other than everyone still eating the room has been extremely quiet.

"Did you have fun with Amber today?" Fire asks me breaking the silence but also ignoring the two brothers looking her way.

"Oh yes. I had a lot of fun with her. She's such a sweet little girl. And so well mannered which is rare in one so young."

"Well she's had only her mother's influence in her life. No telling how she'd be if her dad was around." She says as she slowly looks back at Reaper who has a tight grip on the glass in his hand that I am surprised it hasn't yet shattered.

"That's a shame really. I think a child needs the influence of both parents to help them learn their way through this crazy world." I answer softly.

"If only it were that simple." Fire says just as softly back to me before finishing her plate of food. A few minutes later, Reaper slowly gets up from the table and walks towards his room without ever eating a single bite or saying another word. Spark watches him leave with a pitying look on his face.

Once Reaper is out of the room, Spark turns toward Fire asking, "Why the hell have you not told me she was here? Not only that, how the hell have you hidden the fact that Reaper has a fucking daughter?"

"If he wanted to know that he had one, he would have come looking wouldn't he? So don't go yelling at me for your brother's fuck up! This whole damn situation is screwed up and it's his fucking fault!" She screams at him before shoving away from the table and walking out.

Spark seems to deflate in that moment, just sitting back in his chair, rubbing the back of his neck. He finally says to the room, "Sorry we interrupted everyone's dinner."

"Don't worry about it. What's a family meal without a little family drama?" Officer Wilson replies making the rest of the room start to laugh. After that, conversations resumed around the room and everything was back to normal.

After supper while Bella helps to clean up, I head outside. Reaper is leaning against the outside of the shop when I come out, so I head in his direction.

"Hey man, sorry if Bella and I stepped on your toes by watching Amber today." I say as I light up a smoke.

"No worries man. I didn't even know that Jade lived here and I certainly didn't know anything about Amber. Fuck! This changes things." He says as he rubs the back of his neck.

"Well," I say as I slap him on the shoulder, "Guess I should be the first to congratulate you on being a dad."

At first he looks at me with a shocked expression that soon turns into a huge grin.

"Holy hell, I always thought being told that would scare the shit out of me."

"And now?" I ask but already know the answer based on the look on his face.

"Now I am thinking she is the cutest kid I have ever seen. But I am also thinking I have some stuff to get worked out between her mother and I before we leave New Orleans. And that is going to be a bit tricky. I'll see ya later." He says as he walks away seeming distracted.

A few minutes later I see a car pull along side the front gate. It continues to just sit there but as I begin to walk in that direction, the car starts up again and continues on down the street.

Was probably just someone who had lost their way but to be sure, I'll tell Buzz so that he can pull the security feed. I look back at the road one last time before I head inside.

"Something wrong Blade?" Skeeter says from just inside the door where he sees me looking back at the street,

"Not sure. A car pulled up at the gate and sat there for a few minutes. When I started in its direction, it continued down the street. Figured I'd tell Buzz and he could check the security feed. Run the license plate or something just in case."

"With everything that we are in the middle of at the moment, that would be a good idea. Tell him to get right on it. Would hate for it to be something to do with the warehouse and the girls that could mess everything to hell."

"Right." I answer as I head towards the computer room.

"Hey man. What's up?" Buzz says as a way of greeting as I walk into the room.

"There was a car that pulled up at the gate a few minutes ago. When I walked towards it, they moved on. Skeeter and I both thought it a good idea to get you to look at the video feeds and see if there's a clear picture of the plates."

"I'll pull it up right now." He says as he turns toward one of his computers and starts clicking buttons. "Here we go." He says as I see the footage come up on the screen. "I'll run the plate numbers and let you both know what I find."

"Thanks man." I say as I head out the door in search of my sweet little Pixie.

I finally track her down in our room and can hear her in the shower. There is no way I am missing a chance to see my girl all wet and naked!

"Oh Jesus! Just scare someone into a heart attack why don't you!" She exclaims as I open the shower door.

Just the sight of her has my cock instantly hard and I shoot her a grin.

"Well, don't die on me just yet. I have plans for that soapy wet body." I reply scanning her from head to toe. And damn if those toes aren't just as pretty as the rest of her. Wonder if she'd let me suck on them? I certainly plan on it.

I pull her to me as I shut the shower door, kissing her and pressing my cock into her stomach.

"God, you always taste so good my sweet pixie. I can't wait for you this time. I need you too fucking bad right now!"

I lift her by her thighs and back her into the shower wall. I lift her up a little more to line my cock up with her pussy and slam home in one quick thrust. Her pussy instantly starts to spasm, letting me know it won't take much to send her over the ledge as well.

"Already so wet for my cock. Were you in here thinking about me? Maybe touching yourself while you think of me fucking you?" I ask as I hold perfectly still.

"Oh my God Blade, just fuck me!"

"You will answer my questions first sweet Pixie. You already know I can wait you out." I say as I grin at her.

"Yes Blade, I was rubbing my clit and thinking about you fucking me against this very wall." She replies in the sexiest voice I have ever heard.

I immediately start fucking her hard. As I get closer to climax, I reach down and pinch her clit making her orgasm at the same time as I do.

She is so spent that I don't put her down. I just reach turning off the water and walk us both to the bed.

"We didn't dry off." She says as way of a protest.

"The bed will survive. I'm not done with you yet." I say as I lay her face down on the bed. "Pull your legs up under you and stick your ass up for me."

Before she is even completely in position, my face is buried in her cunt and ass making her moan. I move my index finger to the ring of her ass just barely pushing in.

"I'm going to take you here Bella. Are you ready?"

"Oh yes, please Blade!" she says as she wiggles.

I reach to the bedside table and grab a bottle of lube I got one of the prospects to pick up for me in town. I rub her ass in it and my cock as well. I kneel behind her, lining my cock up with her ass and slowly push the head inside.

"Ugh fuck Blade! Give me more!"

"Reach down and play with your clit my love." I instruct as I slowly push even further inside until I am fully seated to the hilt.

I hold still letting her get used to me here again. Its been months since I have taken her this way. I want to fill her every hole with my cum, marking her with my scent. I know it sounds barbaric but I make no apologies for how fucked up I am.

When I feel her begin to loosen up and relax, I start a slow steady rhythm. Her breathing picks up and she begins to spasm on my cock the way she does before she orgasms.

"Rub that pussy faster baby and make us both explode!" I grunt out as the room fills with the sounds of my hips slapping her ass.

"Oh shit!" she exclaims as I reach around her and pinch her nipples. I feel like my cock is caught in a vice that feels like velvet as we both explode and collapse to the bed still connected together.

I pull her into my arms and lay snuggled to her until my cock goes soft allowing me to pull out of her easily. She barely moves as her breathing slows letting me know that she has fallen asleep.

Ten minutes later, I am almost asleep myself when there is a knock at the bedroom door. I gently unwrap myself from Bella and get out of bed. I've barely gotten my jeans pulled up when I open the door to see who it is.

"Got some information on that car from earlier. Skeeter asked me to come get you." Buzz says.

"I'll be right there." I reply before shutting the door back.

I get completely dressed and gently kiss Bella on top of her head. She barely opens her eyes looking at me.

"Where are you going?" She asks.

"Have a meeting with Skeeter. I'll be back shortly. Get you some rest, beautiful." I answer kissing her softly on her lips before turning and walking to the door. I look back at her before walking out and see that she is already back to sleep.

Heading into the computer room, I see that Reaper is also here.

"Did it come back as one of the guys from the warehouse?" I ask immediately.

"Actually, no it didn't." Skeeter replies.

"It's actually someone we ran across in Memphis. Where we found Bella." Reaper says while looking at a picture on one of Buzz's computers.

"Are you implying she was with this guy while away from me?" I quietly ask.

"Not at all but he was kind of manhandling her when I spotted her from across the room. She said he was someone that didn't seem to want to take no for an answer." Reaper replies.

"And it looks like he still isn't taking no for an answer if he's followed her all the way down here." Buzz says with granite in his voice.

"Guess I should pay him a little visit. Do we know where he is staying at?" I ask Buzz but Skeeter replies.

"It's already taken care of. He should be delivered to the shed out back here shortly."

"Good. Text me when he's ready. I need to go talk to my girl first." I say as I head back towards the bedroom.

As I walk in, I look at my sweet girl while she sleeps. I know she deserves better than me. I'm more than fucked in the head.

The thought of that weaselly looking fucker having his hands on her has the monster inside of me in a rage. I've got to calm down before dealing with him or I will just put a fast bullet into his head.

As a club we might be going all legal and shit but we will still put your ass six feet under for messing with our family. Bella is my family and by extension, she's part of the MC family.

I strip off my clothes and gently start pulling the blankets down off her body.

Bella

I wake up to Blade kissing my lower back just above the curve of my butt. My body already ignited into a burning inferno. I have only ever responded to him. It makes no sense at all. Even back when we were younger I could look at him and I could feel sparks igniting inside of me.

It was never that way with any of the other boys around town. My very first orgasm was by my own hand and with him in my minds eye.

I can't stop the moan as his tongue glides over my crack all the way to the junction of my thighs. He rolls me over to my back and immediately latches onto my clit.

"Ugh!" I exclaim as a whole new feeling spreads down to my toes. I'm not expecting it when he suddenly stops causing me to protest.

"What are you doing?" I ask breathlessly.

"I have questions my love." He says with serious eyes looking back at me.

"What are you talking about? I am so close!" I say as I try but fail to pull his head back down to my throbbing pussy.

"I'll ask the questions and then you'll get what you want." He says with a devilish smile and I throw my head back against the pillow to wait for his questions. The man is made to drive me crazy.

"Hurry up and ask dammit!" I say looking back down at him when he takes longer than needed to start talking.

He looks at me a moment longer before he says, "You know what? I don't need to ask when I already know."

I'm about to ask what he's talking about again but before I am able to get a word out, he latches onto my clit again, sucking even harder. It sends me into an automatic climax that curls my damn toes so hard that I no longer can feel them.

He slides up my body slamming his cock inside of me in one hard thrust. He feels so big and so good that I feel like I should be purring.

I wrap my legs around his waist as he holds both my hands above my head with one hand and the other hand grabs one of my nipples rolling it around. Giving me the sense of both pleasure and pain.

"I can feel your pussy throbbing sweet Bella. Cum on this cock! I want to feel those walls squeezing the life out of my balls!" He grunts out as he pumps himself even faster in and out of me.

"Oh fuck Blade! Harder baby!" I beg.

"Yes my love, just like that! Cum for me! Do it now!" He demands of me.

Just like that I explode into a million pieces just as I feel him swell even bigger inside of me and warmth coats my insides.

Chapter 7

Blade

An hour later I leave Bella sleeping again as I head out back to the shed to deal with the fucker that has followed my girl here. Reaper is standing next to the door waiting for me.

"One of the prospects has already brought your bag out. What exactly is your plan here?" Reaper asks.

"He hasn't really done anything other than following her." Skeeter says as he walks up.

"I just want to make it clear that she is off limits and for him to go his ass back North where the fuck he belongs." I answer as we head inside and shut the door.

I can see the asshole sitting in a chair that the guys have tied him to. He also has a gag in his mouth. I walk over, grabbing myself a chair and sitting in front of of him.

His eyes seem to be unfocused. That could be because they are both nearly swelled shut. Guess the guys roughed him up a bit for me first which puts a crazy grin on my face.

"Wake up jackass!". I slap his face a few times to help him focus a little. "So you like to stalk women across state lines when they have repeated told you to leave them alone."

"They all say no when they actually mean yes." He says as he starts to laugh but before I even realize what I am doing, one of my knives is in my hand with the blade barely against his jaw.

Its so sharp that it has already started to draw blood and he immediately stops moving at all.

"I bet you think this face gets you every thing you want, including women that do not want you. What if I change it for you? Make it even more pretty. I could even replace it with another one. My stitches would be so flawless no one would ever know you had a different face." I say as fear replaces the look in his eyes.

"Blade..." I hear from behind me and I slowly move my knife away.

"You will leave and you will not follow or even try to contact Bella again. If you do, we will know. And I will remove your face for you. Understand?" I say to the asshole sitting in front of me.

"You're the one that doesn't understand." He says with a raspy voice.

"Then explain it to me mother fucker."

"Sweet little Bella was hand selected. She will spawn the purest blood that will give us new life."

I look into his eyes while he is saying this and I can see that he completely believes in whatever the fuck he is talking about.

"I was charged with bringing her home. Lucky for me, your friends brought her for me." He says with a smile just before screaming as I push my blade into his left cheek. Its time to get answers and this mother fucker knows way more than   he   has   said.

Bella

The next day all the guys are busy with all of their plans. From what I have over heard, they will attack the warehouse tonight. Blade won't talk to me about it. Keeps telling me that its club business and for me not to worry. But I worry anyway.

Being back with him this time has caused me to see how very much I love him. It has also caused me to see that I should trust him more, not make assumptions without talking to him first.

And I want babies, with him. Sweet little boys and tiny little girly girl babies. All of them with eyes the same shade as his. The way that we have been with each other since I've gotten here and the fact that I have not been taking my pill, it wouldn't surprise me if we are already expecting. Just the thought makes me giddy. Blade will be an amazing dad.

I am walking through the bar area towards the kitchen when Fire comes through the door.

"Hey girl!" She says with a smile on her face.

"Hey. What's got you in such a good mood?" I ask and watch as her face turns red as if she is blushing.

"Looks like I am going back home with my husband after all of this is over." She replies.

"That's certainly something worth smiling about."

"It is and I have missed him. Besides, what ever is between Reaper and Jade they need to work out on their own. I should have never let any of it come between Spark and I." She says.

"Yeah I think I too am learning that I need to trust Blade more than I have so far."

"He does love you, ya know? When he first got here and you were missing, he looked like a man that had lost his favorite toy." She says as she chuckles.

"Should I be offended that you just called me a toy?" I ask with mock outrage.

"Not at all. Because if I didn't like you I'd have called you something else." She replies and we both bust out laughing.

The door from outside opens again as we are still laughing together and someone else walks in.

"Well look at you two bitches!" We both turn towards the voice and see Mina standing there.

"Oh my God!!" Fire and I say at the same time as we rush over to Mina and hug her.

"I'm so glad you are here! But you could have at least told me you were coming!" I say to her.

"I didn't even know we were coming until I realized Timber wasn't turning around as we left town!" she replies

"That sounds just like all our men." Fire says and we all bust into laughter.

"So, where's Jade and my niece?" Mina asks Fire.

"They should be here shortly. When I left her place earlier, your brother was camped out on the doorstep."

"What I wouldn't give to be a fly on that wall." Mina replies. "She shouldn't have kept Amber to herself like that."

"Yeah, I know. I kept hoping I could get her to go back home with me. But she's as stubborn as a damn mule."

"I heard that!" Jade says from the door as her and Amber walk in with Reaper right behind them.

"Well, she's right. You are stubborn as hell!" Reaper says as he sets Amber's bag down on a nearby table, bends down to talk to her a minute before walking back towards the room all the other guys have been in this morning.

"I hate that man!" she mumbles as she watches him walk away.

"No you don't. You have loved him since you were twelve. I should know. I was there." Mina says, making Fire start to laugh but covers her mouth trying to hold it in.

We all watch as Jade, who is now offended, walk over to her daughter and sit down with her. The rest of us head towards the kitchen to get something to eat.

85

Blade

We have all been rushing around planning and prepping everything that we can in hopes of tonight going smoothly. We all want to get those women out of there without anything else happening to them. They've been through enough.

The information I was able to extract from that mother fucker last night was enough to make us all want to jump ahead and get to those poor women in that warehouse.

By seven in the evening we have everything ready and head into the clubhouse to drink a few beers. We have time to pass as we are not planning to hit the warehouse until midnight.

Reaper, Spark, Timber and myself walk in grabbing chairs and pulling them up to sit with our girls who are all at the same table.

"You guys heading out soon?" Mina asks.

"Soon enough. Come dance with me woman!" Timber replies as he pulls her from her chair into his arms.

I look over at my girl wondering if she's happy. She tried to run away from me before and it scared the absolute shit out of me. She just doesn't get that I really do need her. I will always need her.

She's like the air I need to breathe just to feel human. If she knew the things I was capable of doing, she probably would run again and never let me within a hundred miles of her.

I lean over and kiss her just behind her ear as I whisper, "I really do love you so very much."

She turns to look me and I see a tear starting to form in her eyes. "I really do love you too, Blade. I always have."

I pick my girl up and move her to my lap just to hold her. I'm absolutely certain I haven't ever been this happy in my life.

"I want babies Bella. I want them with you and no one else. Losing that baby destroyed me. I blamed myself for not getting to you fast enough."

"It wasn't your fault anymore than it was mine Blade. I've learned the past few months that things happen. Sometimes good things and sometimes bad things. We just have to ride the waves of life and learn from what happens along the way."

"You can't run away like that again either. Not knowing where you were, If you were safe or getting enough to eat. I couldn't concentrate on anything else."

"I promise that I won't. I'm exactly where I want to be."

"In my lap?" I reply with a wicked grin as I move a little bit so she can feel that I am already hard for her. Talking about or thinking about babies with my girl does that to me.

"Wherever you are." She giggles out as she pushes down on me.

"Damn woman." I groan out as I jump up and drag her towards our room.

She's pissed off at me but I don't give a shit. The damn woman ran off, had my kid and never fucking told me about it. Not only that, but I have been looking for her this entire time and her fucking sister knew exactly where she was. So yeah, I'm pissed off at everyone.

"Want something else to drink?" I ask.

"If I did, I can get it my damn self." Jade replies back but still not looking at me.

I reach over putting my arm around her and pulling her close until my lips are next to her ear.

"You will talk to me respectfully or I will take you to the back and spank your little ass like I did the night you snuck into my room." I say causing her to gasp and also turn a pretty shade of pink.

"I thought you didn't remember that night."

"I thought I had dreamed it. But now that I know about Amber, small bits and pieces are coming back to me."

"So now that you know, you're going to kidnap us and make us go back home with you?"

"You are mine Jade. You have always been mine. I know it. You know it. You knew it the night you snuck into my room."

"That's bullshit. You only want me now because of Amber."

"That's where you'd be wrong. You know I've been searching for you. It's why you've kept jobs that only pay you cash and working towards your teachers degree online.”

She gives me a look of surprise. Guess she thought I wouldn’t know about her going to school.

“You can apply for a job at the school when we get you both settled back in at home.”

“I don’t plan on us being there that long.” She replies as she pulls away from me.

“I suggest you plan again.” I growl back as I sit back in my chair and drink my beer.

Jade

After that conversation with Reaper at the table, I excused myself to go to the restroom. I'm shaking so bad from anger I am afraid I might break a beer bottle over the top of his head.

He's not the only one I am pissed off at. My own sister in the past few days has seemed to turn against me and be on his side. I'm so focused on thinking about everything that I don't hear the door open.

"Still pissed off I see." My sister says from just inside the door.

"I'm not speaking to you!"

"Stop being a damn baby Jade! That man had every right to know about his daughter and you know it! Hell, I should have told him when I finally found your ass last year!"

"Then why didn't you?"

"Because that is something he should have heard from you Jade. Despite the fact that I hate his fucking guts, I know that he loves you. Hell we've all known he was in love with you since you were sixteen."

"I thought he was for a long time too. I thought he was just waiting until I was old enough. But on my birthday when I turned eighteen, he stayed away. Didn't pay me any attention at all.

That's why a week later I snuck into his bedroom. But the days after it was like it never even happened. I finally walked in one afternoon

90

and kissed him straight on the mouth. In front of some of the guys." I reply starting to cry.

"The day you left?"

"Yes. That was the day I left. After I kissed him, he pushed me away and told me I was just a kid. For me to behave myself. So I packed up my car and started driving. I stayed in Gulf Shores for a while. That's where I was when I found out I was pregnant with Amber."

My sister pulls me into a hug and I cry even harder.

"Give him a chance to make things right Jade. Trust me when I tell you that he is most definitely in love with you. It's why he got so pissy when Spark and I got married."

I pull back looking at her and ask, "Did you really set fire to the cabin?"

She shakes her head, "I damn sure did. He was passed out on the couch. You should have seen it. It was beautiful. A grown man, completely nude, running around trying to put out the blaze with a waterhose." She explains with this crazy look in her eye.

"Girl, you have a serious issue with fire. Please do not teach that to Amber." I say as we both bust out laughing.

Chapter 8

Bella

The guys have been gone for an hour and I am a nervous wreak. I hope they all stay safe and none of them get seriously hurt. I keep checking my phone although I know that we won't know anything until they all get back.

I'm sitting at the table listening to the other girls talk as my phone starts ringing with a call from my mom. It's later than she is usually up so I am worried when I answer.

"Mom? Everything okay?"

"Everything is fine with me sweetheart. I didn't mean to worry you by calling at this hour."

"It's fine. What's up?"

"I got a call from a lawyer in Mobile Alabama about your cousin Shay. Not sure if you remember her but she's my sister's only daughter."

"Yeah I remember her. Last I heard she was real bad on drugs and lived somewhere around New York or something."

"That was the last I heard too. But this lawyer says she had been staying in Mobile for several months now. That she got clean."

"Okay, that's good. So what's he calling you for?"

"Actually he was calling for you. Shay died in child birth. She never named a father. She probably didn't even know who it was. But that lawyer says she named you as the guardian of her son." She says giving me a shock.

"What? But why me?" I whisper. The other girls have all gone quiet as I am sure they know something serious is happening.

"Well sweetheart, we are the only family the girl had left. And you two used to be thick as thieves when you were younger. Back before she went wild that is. You should call him. Check on the baby. Find out what she named him. I didn't think to ask Mr Francis."

"Text me the number and I will call him before it gets too much later."

"I will sweetheart. Let me know what all you find out. I love you."

"I love you too momma. Bye." I say as I hang up.

"Girl what is up?" Mina asks.

"My cousin Shay died. She had a baby and she named me as guardian. I'm supposed to call this lawyer back soon as mom sends me the number."

"Damn. How old is the baby?" Fire asks.

"I'm not sure. Mom said she died during childbirth so I'm guessing only a few days old." I answer as a text from mom comes through my phone. "She just sent me his number."

"Go call him. Find out what is going on." Says Mina as I get up from the table and head to the bedroom where it is quieter.

Blade

My wrath is stronger than my mercy. Flashes of memory of what Bella looked like when we finally got to her run rampant in my head.

I'm covered in sweat, dirt and blood by the time we make it into the warehouse. We spread out and sweep each area as we go, taking down those that lay down their weapons quietly. But there have been plenty who have been given an award of a single bullet between the eyes.

"Thanks for getting that last asshole back there." I say to Officer Wilson.

"Not a problem son. I kind of like you with your head intact." He says laughing a little and causing me to grunt in return. I kinda like having my head in one piece too.

"Officer Wilson! We need you inside!" Timber calls from the side entrance door.

As we walk in, carefully stepping over a few bodies, we can see Timber walking down a hallway where we know the women have been kept and waiting for us by a door on the right.

"We are pretty sure your niece is in this room. She doesn't know any of us so I need you to go in and try to calm her." Timber says to Officer Wilson as he opens the door to let him in.

We stay by the door and watch as Officer Wilson fails to calm her enough to get close to her. She just keeps screaming.

Our Sergeant at Arms, Blood, who had been standing quietly in the corner apparently had

95

enough and walked straight to her bed and picked her up. He whispers quietly in her ear and she stops screaming.

"We can go now." Blood says to the rest of us as he walks out with Miranda still wrapped tightly in his arms.

"That was weird." I say as I watch the big guy carry her out.

"Weird or not, I'm ready to get out of this stink hole." Timber says.

"What will happen to the rest of the women." Officer Wilson asks.

"We will make sure they get the hospital care they need and back to their families," Agent Richards says. "We never could have done any of this without your clubs. Any of you thought about doing private contract work?"

"What do you mean?" Reaper asks.

"Sometimes there are jobs that require a little more than our government is technically allowed. If you know what I mean."

"Hmm. Maybe it is something we can talk more detail about over a beer at the Night Howler's club house?" Says Skeeter who looks at the other club Presidents for their okay as well.

"I will need you to come to Mobile as soon as you can to go over everything with you. Your cousin was very adamant that you also bring along Mr. Chester Whiteson as he plays a key role in what needs to be done as well."

"Blade? What on earth could she have wanted him there for?" I ask.

"I am not at liberty to discuss all the details over the phone Miss Winters. Do you know when you two could be here?"

"I would need to talk with Blade first to be sure but would 2pm tomorrow be okay?" I ask.

"That time will be just fine. I look forward to meeting you both then." He replies just before he hangs up.

As I'm walking back out to the bar area where I left the girls, I can hear the guys coming back. I run straight to Blade as he comes through the door and wrap my arms around him.

"I'm covered in blood and dirty beautiful."

"Is the blood from you?" I ask as I push him back at arms length to look him over good.

"Nah, I'm not hurt baby." He says to me with that slightly crooked smile he gives me when he thinks I'm being cute.

"If you call me cute right this minute, I'm going to punch you in the nose." I say to him with as serious a face as I can.

"God, I love you." He says while laughing at me. "Let me go get a shower and I'll meet you at the bar."

Just then the doors open and Blood from the Wolfsbane Ridge MC walks through holding a really bloody woman with Officer Wilson trailing behind him.

"Was that Officer Wilson's niece?" I ask Blade.

"Yes. She looked so broken and wouldn't stop screaming. Not even when Officer Wilson went to her. Blood just walked up and picked her up. Said something quietly to her and it was like all the air left her sails. Hasn't made a peep since." He says as he looks down the hall they all disappeared down.

"Go get a shower honey. I have something to talk to you about while we eat." I say as I kiss him and walk back to my friends.

Walk back to the table and sit with Mina. They are currently talking about the girl that Blood brought in and carried to a room.

"She is going to need a lot of help and support for everything she has gone through." Mina says.

"There is no telling what all they did to her. What I went through couldn't possibly compare to the months of torture she has gone through." I say to the table.

"We will be there for her." Mina says as she grabs my hand with a sad smile.

I run into Timber in the hall after getting my shower and we go to the computer room to meet up with the rest of the guys.

"So far from what we have gathered, some of the girls were used as baby making machines." We hear Agent Richards saying to Skeeter as we walk into the room.

"What the fuck do you mean?" I ask.

"They needed babies for the black market. Some are sold to couples who are seriously looking to have a child and some sold for nefarious reasons."

"As for some of the other women, their body parts were being harvested and sold. The women that were in the room with Miss Grayson were there simply for the use of the cult that is behind all of it. Until one of the women is able to talk fully with us, we really won't know what all they have gone through." He explains to the room of quiet bikers.

"Can Miranda go back home with us?" Blood speaks up to ask causing our President and Officer Wilson to look at him oddly. Which in turn causes Blood to fidget under their scrutiny.

"As long as her doctor says she is okay to travel she can go where she wants. If my department has any questions for her, I know who to contact." He says tilting his head in Timber's direction.

A little while later I find Bella at a table with the rest of the girls. She has a huge smile on her face and it is amazing to see. After her kidnapping that resulted in the loss of our baby, I was afraid I would never see her smile like that again.

"What are you over there grinning at handsome?" she asks as she stands up and walks toward me.

"You. You are so beautiful when your smile reaches your eyes." I reply and kiss her on her nose causing her to giggle.

"So what is it you needed to talk to me about?" I ask.

"Well, I got a call from a lawyer in Mobile, Alabama."

"Why is a lawyer calling you?" I ask coming completely alert and afraid something is wrong.

"You remember my cousin Shay?" she asks.

"Of course I do. You two were thick as thieves when you were younger. I still haven't forgotten the frogs the two of you put in the saddle bags on my first bike. I almost wreaked when one jumped out onto my back while driving down the road." I say trying not to laugh at the memory.

"You have to admit that shit was fucking funny. I almost wreaked my bike from laughing at your ass freaking out over a green tree from." Timber says over hearing our conversation.

"Anyway," Bella says while rolling her eyes. "She passed away a few days ago during childbirth. The lawyer says she did not say who the father was. Only that he was to contact both of us. He called you Mr Chester Whiteson." She says with a giggle. "I told him we could be at his office tomorrow at 2pm. Is that okay?"

"Yeah that shouldn't be a problem." I reply looking at Timber for confirmation.

"We will ride with you two. That way we all can head back home together." He says.

"Thanks man." I say.

"No problem, Mr Chester." He says as he slaps my shoulder.

"You're an asshole and I have no idea why I have stayed friends with you over the years." I say to his retreating back.

Chapter 9
Bella

We arrived in Mobile around lunch time. The guys wanted to get there early enough to stop for something to eat. The plan was to leave most of the guys at the restaurant to wait for us to be done at the lawyers office. However; none of them wanted to wait there when they found out that my cousin had a baby that may be coming back home with us.

"We have an appointment with Mr. Francis." I say to the receptionist. She looks up and her eyes get huge watching all the bikers that file in behind me.

"Yes. Umm, Mr Francis should be here directly. He asked me to show you to the meeting room." She replies as she begins walking down a hall and looks back to be sure we are all following her.

"There is water and coffee on the table in the corner." She says as she leaves us in the room.

"She's a little jumpy." Blood says to the rest of us.

"When you are not used to bikers, I imagine watching a crowd of them coming into the room can be intimidating." Mina says as she takes a seat.

Less than ten minutes later the door opens and we watch a man I assume to be Mr. Francis walking.

"Sorry for being a tad bit late. Which of you young ladies is Miss Winter?" He asks.

"That would be me." I speak up.

"Yes, I can see now the resemblance to Miss Shay." He says with a sad smile. "And which of you gentlemen is Mr. Whiteson?"

"I prefer being called Blade."

"Yes, so sorry. Miss Shay did mention that to me. Let's get started shall we?" He says as he sits down and begins pulling out papers from his briefcase.

"Miss Shay contacted me several months ago and hired me as her lawyer. She knew she was dying and wanted to be sure that her child would be taken care of after her passing. She was very adamant about him not going into the system." He begins to explain.

"What exactly does this have to do with me? She was Bella's cousin and not exactly close to me at." Blade asks.

"I'm trying to get to that. You see, she knew that her cousin would be the best mother for her son but she wanted to be sure that he also had a father he could look up to. Those were her exact words. From what I gathered from talking with her over he last months, she didn't have the best home life while growing us. As I recall she called her father an abusive drunken prick." He says.

"She wants me to be this child's father?" Blade asks with wonder in his voice.

"Yes, that is exactly what Miss Shay wanted. She left you both each a letter. She asked that you wait to open it until the day the adoption becomes final."

"So what do we need to do? Just sign a few papers and that's it? We can take him home?" I ask.

"Yes that is pretty much it. When we finish here, I can go with you to the hospital to show proof to the two of you being the new parents so you can take him home."

"Does he have a name yet?" asks Blade.

"No, she left that up to the two of you. She said that as the parents you should have all the say in everything including his name." Mr. Francis replies as he pushes a stack of papers towards us. "If the two of you would sign at the bottom of each page, we can finish this up and go pick up your new son." He says with a smile.

Almost two hours later we are in a private room at the hospital waiting for the nurse to bring in the baby.

"I can't believe she's gone and left her baby to us." Bella says with tears in her eyes.

"I am so sorry about Shay. I wish she had come back to Montana instead of dying alone here. She was a sweet girl when you two were little." I say to her.

"So who is first? Mom or dad?" asks a nurse who is walking through the door holding a baby wrapped in a blue blanket.

"You hold him first Blade." Bella says with a watery smile.

As the nurse lays him in my arms and I get my first good look at his sweet tiny face, a strange feeling comes over me.

"His name should be Justice." I say to Bella.

"That is actually perfect. She used to dream of being a huge lawyer." She says as she begins to quietly cry.

"Yeah, I remember picking on her about it. I wish that dream had come true for her." I say.

"Me too." She says as she sits on the arm of the chair to stare down at our son, Justice.

We've been back home nearly a week. Blade has been staying every night at my house with Justice and myself. We haven't really talked about him moving in completely but I do think it is headed that way.

I yawn again as I refill the salt shakers.

"My new grandson keeping you up or is it that beautiful man keeping you up by setting your panties on fire?" My mom asks while wiggling her eyebrows.

"Seriously, mom? You shouldn't even think about that kind of thing." I say with a grossed out look on my face.

"What? I may be your mom but I am not dead." She says as she carries dirty dishes to the back.

I'm still looking toward where my mom went when Mina comes through the front door.

"Hey girl! Why do you look like you don't know if you should scream or puke?" she asks me.

"My mom." I say with a shake of my head knowing that is the only explanation that Mina needs.

"Where's baby Justice?" she asks.

"Blade came by earlier and picked him up. Give me a little time to catch up on office work and everything."

"He is really a great dad." Mina says.

"Yes he really is." I say wistfully thinking about our baby that was lost.

"Hey. What's meant to be will be." Mina says while grabbing my hand.

"Did you get that thing I asked you to get for me?" I ask her.

"Yes I did." She says as she hands me a bag. "You going to do it here or at home later?" she asks.

"Now. I don't want him to catch me at the house later." I say as I walk towards the bathroom.

Ten minutes later I am sitting in my office with Mina.

"I'm excited but scared out of my damn mind Mina!!"

"He or she will be close in age with Justice. It's perfect if you ask me." She says giggling at my shell shocked face.

Finally after a few more minutes of over reacting I start laughing. I can't stop and the harder I try the harder I laugh. Mina starts laughing with me and this is how the men find us. Laughing so hard we are about to pee in our pants. The looks on their face causes another hard round of laughing.

"What the fuck is wrong with them?" Timber asks.

"How the fuck should I know. You and I came in together." Blade says back to him.

"There is nothing wrong with us!" Mina says as she stands up.

"You ready to go baby?" Timber asks her.

"I'll see you later Bella. Let me know how everything goes. Oh, and you two don't forget about the party Friday night to welcome the newest little member!" She says to me as they leave.

"What did she mean about letting her know how everything goes?" Blade asks after they leave.

"I'll tell you later. I'm ready to go home, get a shower and eat supper. I'm exhausted and my feet are killing me." I say with a smile.

"I thought we might order from that Chinese place you like so much." Blade says as he picks up the carrier holding Justice and we walk out to my car.

I'm setting out our supper while waiting for Bella to come down after her shower. She's been acting a little weird since I picked her up from work. It has me nervous.

What if she has noticed me slowly leaving stuff here in her house and doesn't want me moving in? Or worse case, she has decided she doesn't want me any more. There is just no way I could share children with her, live in the same town and watch as she moves on with someone else later. Hell fucking no. That will never happen.

"Hmm. That smells so good. Did you get me the beef pepper steak?" She asks as she sits down at the table.

"Yes baby, I knew it was your favorite." I say as I sit down and begin fixing a plate.

We eat in silence for several minutes until I can't stand it any more.

"SO what is it? What is wrong? Do you not want me here?" I ask.

"What are you talking about? Of course I want you here." She says.

"You've acted strange all evening." I say back.

"Well I have something to tell you." Her face says it is something really serious. She straightens her back in her chair.

"We are pregnant." She says.

"Yeah well, I already knew that. I thought you were going to say I couldn't move in here with you."

She looks at me as if I have two heads and she isn't sure yet which one she'll cut off.

"How do you already know that I am pregnant?"

"I was around for the first one Bella. Its not hard to tell with you. Certain smells make you sick from the very beginning. I'd say you aren't very far along just yet because the puking hasn't started." I say on a laugh that I quickly swallow as I am sure her eyes are shooting death at me.

"Sometimes I really don't like you!" she exclaims as she takes her plate to the sink.

"BUT you still love me!" I say back before fixing myself another plate.

Chapter 10

Blade

"So Skeeter and his crew are going to work with the government?" I ask Timber during church.

"Most of his club are ex-military so it makes since they'd jump at this chance. As for us, we have some new custom orders that came in through the shop.

Also, I need all of you out spreading the word about the fund raiser. Get the girls out there to help pass out fliers. I want to make sure we raise enough money to get every kid in our town that can't afford one a bicycle of his or her own this year for Christmas. Does anyone have anything else to add?" Timber says to the room.

"I need Officer Wilson to stop hounding Miranda about leaving the club house." Blood says out loud.

"It makes sense that he would want to take her home Blood. She's his niece." Timber explains.

"She's mine and ain't leaving." He says crossing his arms like a child fighting to keep his favorite toy.

"What do you mean she's yours?" Timber asks slowly as if even he's afraid of the answer.

"I saved her. Until she feels better, she stays with me."

"I'll talk to Officer Wilson but Blood, if and when that girls says she wants to leave, I will

113

give her a ride any where she wishes to go. Are we clear? You do not need to form any type of attachment to her. She's not like the girls you fuck for a night and send packing the next." Timber says as if he were talking to a child.

I don't know of anyone else that could get away with talking to Blood that way. The man is huge. He's also a major asshole but the ladies seem to love him.

"Don't forget about the family party tomorrow night to welcome our newest member to our MC family. If that is all, Church is dismissed."

I sit and watch everyone else file out of the room.

"What do you think has gotten into Blood?" I ask Timber.

"Hell, I don't know. Do you remember several months ago when the fool was walking around here talking about seeing an angel and being lovestruck? Then a little bit later he was back to being his asshole self?"

"I think I remember that. Is that when he changed the locks on his door to keep the yotes out of his room because he said his body belonged only to the Angel?" I ask laughing at the memory.

"Yep. And I do believe that we now know that Angel to be none other than Miranda Grayson."

"Holy shit! Not too sure how that will go over with Officer Wilson." I reply as we walk out of the room.

"Do you really think you'll need all of this tonight? It's just a family party." Blade says to me as he picks up the three different diaper bags I packed for Justice.

"With babies you never know what all they may need. One bag has a change of clothes in case of an accident along with diapers and wipes. One bag has his paste for his butt so he doesn't get a rash, powder, an extra blanket and a few toys. The other has his bottles and formula." I explain with a roll of my eyes.

"I guess we won't be taking very many trips until he's potty trained then. This is way too much shit." He complains but carries the bags inside the clubhouse.

As we walk in, there's a huge banner hanging from the ceiling that says welcome to the family as well as blue balloons floating around everywhere. Once we are noticed, everyone begins to clap a cheer while congratulating us.

"Okay, okay, everyone settle down." Timber says, waiting for everyone to get quiet.

"As you all my already know, Bella's cousin, Shay, passed away leaving behind a sweet little boy. Her dying wish was for Bella along with Blade, to raise the child as their own. They have named him Justice in memory of the Shay we all used to know." Timber says talking to the entire room.

"We all offer the two of you our congratulations and welcome little Justice to our MC family."

"Thank you everyone. I also would like to let everyone know that we are expecting another child." As soon as Blade speaks, the room erupts into congratulations and back slaps while I stand there with red cheeks.

"Didn't know you were going to tell everyone before we have even seen a doctor." I admonish Blade but lighten it with a sweet kiss.

"I love you, Bella."

"I love you too, Mr. Chester." I say while giggling.

"Hush woman before the other brothers hear you! I would never live it down."

The End

Continue to the following pages for sneak peaks at coming up books by Marissa Ann.

Sneak Peak
Wolfsbane Ridge MC, Book 3
Blood's Angel

Blood

The first time I ever saw Miranda Grayson was in the parking lot of the grocery store. She had her arms full of grocery bags and was having a hard time opening the trunk of her car.

I walked right up, took the bags, opened her trunk, put everything in and walked away. Without every saying a single word. I remember looking back before getting on my bike and seeing a look on her face as if she thought I may be missing a few marbles in my head.

Currently, I'd say she was correct in her assessment. I can't seem to put together a complete sentence in her presence. I'm not sure why her presence has that reaction with me. Quite frankly it pisses me off. I'm not always sure if I want to kill something or just fuck her brains out.

Can you fuck someone until you get them out of your system? I'm not really sure but with her, I'd damn sure be willing to try. But I highly suspect after the first taste of her, I'd never let her go.

Since her kidnapping, I'm not too sure she'd ever let another touch her in that way again. Much less a big ass brute like me that can't talk.

117

Miranda

I've been through hell over this past year but I refuse to allow it to destroy me. They took me from my own home and I am still unsure how exactly they got in. I've not stepped foot back in there since it happened.

Currently I am sharing a room in the Wolfsbane Ridge MC clubhouse with a gorgeous hulk of a man that has rarely spoken two words to me. I should be afraid of him just based on his size. But, oddly, I am comforted by his presence.

I'm sure he'll eventually want me to leave or at least move to a different room. Surely a man like him has a ton of women or maybe even a girlfriend. He wouldn't want to continue to take care of a woman like me. One that is so used up and completely broken.

Uncle John has been by several times already trying to get me to go back home with him. But I am not ready. Especially since he told me that Ray has been by looking for me.

I need to wait until I am stronger. That way I can run because I know if Ray catches me this time, he'll kill me.

Sneak Peak
Night Howler's MC, Book 1
Reaper's Jewels

Reaper

When a man makes a huge dumbass mistake when it comes to the woman he loves, the best thing he can do is force her back home until she forgives him. Right?

It's not like she is the only one with a reason to be pissed the fuck off. She ran off, had MY kid and was never planning to tell me about her. Yeah, I have a daughter now.

This changes things, it changes everything. I don't give a shit what I have to do, I'll pay every dime that weaselly divorce lawyer is trying to get for that bitch I'm married to.

I should have done it three years ago and went after Jade when she left. But I didn't. It was the worst mistake of my life.

Hopefully Jade will forgive me for the last three years. Right now though I think she may want to kill me in my sleep. I didn't give her a choice about going back home.

Jade

He really thinks making me go back to North Mississippi against my will is going to help him win me back. He can go jump off the nearest cliff!

He did want me three years ago. He made that pretty damn plain. Especially when he allowed that bitch to talk to me as if I were just one of the whores that hangs around the club being passed around like a toy.

She had been gone for a couple years and everyone knew Reaper had filed for a divorce. I was so naive to think he was actually in love with me. After what happened that day and the way he acted like she was right about me being nothing to him, I know now, his feelings for me were not that deep.

I have no plans to forgive him. I know he only wants me now because we share a child. Family means everything to the Star family. And now our daughter is a part of that.

Buzz

Several years ago, my little sister was raped and murdered. Her killer was never caught. She had been emailing a guy she had met in an online chat room. Even though the authorities had his name he used online, every lead came to a dead end. It didn't stop me from continuing the search.

A few weeks ago I caught a break. Another programmer I knew from when I was still in the service stumbled across the same name with a different unique IP address that constantly bounces around making it almost impossible to follow.

However, follow it I did and where it winds up leading me has me second guessing what I am planning.

I'll take something of his. His beautiful sister Makayla. But we don't hurt innocents. I will protect her as best I can. I plan on her step brother paying for what he did to my sister with his own blood. What I don't plan for is falling hard for my enemies sister.

Even after all of these years I can't believe my mother was stupid enough to fall for my step father. I have never doubted he had something to do with her disappearance. I've just never been able to prove it.

You would think that with her gone, I'd be free of the Marcus family. Unfortunately for me, my step father adopted me when he married my mother.

My step brother absolutely hates me and I am certain that our Papa is the only one keeping him from doing whatever he wanted to me.

The look I see in his eyes any time I run into him while I am out with friends or a date scares me to my core. I refuse to let him know just how scared of him I really am.

If anything ever happens to Papa or I become expendable in his eyes, I will need to run and run fast. Getting away before he gives me to Joe to do whatever he wants with me, will take a miracle.

More From This Author

https://books2read.com/u/47lz7E

Connect with the Author on Facebook

www.facebook.com/MarissaAnnAuthor/

Or Send her a message through email

marissaann2018@yahoo.com